"First I have to know why you want to marry me."

"I want to marry you so that I have the right to take you to bed whenever I wish, so that I can introduce you as my wife rather than as a kept woman."

"Do I have to decide now?" Dandy asked, wanting to know what had happened to the woman he was in love with but afraid to ask, in case he withdrew from her again.

"Now," Yvan retorted. "I do not want a reluctant, suspicious wife." He seemed to be getting to the end of his patience.

She flung her arms around him. "Yes, I'll marry you."

She would always be his, even though she knew he didn't love her the way he loved Niki. For not once had he said to her *"I love you. I love you very much,"* as he had murmured in his sleep to the woman of his dreams.

Books by Flora Kidd

HARLEQUIN PRESENTS

HARLEQUIN ROMANCE

These books may be available at your local bookseller.

Don't miss any of our special offers. Write to us at the following address for information on our newest releases.

Harlequin Reader Service
P.O. Box 52040, Phoenix, AZ 85072-2040
Canadian address: P.O. Box 2800, Postal Station A,
5170 Yonge St., Willowdale, Ont. M2N 6J3

FLORA KIDD

flight to passion

Harlequin Books

TORONTO • NEW YORK • LONDON
AMSTERDAM • PARIS • SYDNEY • HAMBURG
STOCKHOLM • ATHENS • TOKYO • MILAN

Harlequin Presents first edition March 1985
ISBN 0-373-10771-4

Original hardcover edition published in 1984
by Mills & Boon Limited

CHAPTER ONE

THE day before her wedding day Dandy Kerr Dyer ran away.

She didn't actually run. She drove away in her mother's car, a brand new Mustang, fast and sporty.

The day had started for Dandy, as days so often had started for most of her life, with a mild domestic disaster. Her own car, a Japanese make, given to her for her twenty-first birthday in January by her mother and stepfather, Anne and Morton Dyer, wouldn't start. After spending at least fifteen minutes trying to get it to start Dandy stepped out of the car, slammed the door, gave one of the tyres a kick of frustration and began to walk down the hill to the house on the banks of the Hudson River where her mother lived.

The Dyer house was conical in design. It had tall white columns supporting a portico over an elegant black door. Black shutters contrasted sharply with the white paint of the clapboard siding of the house and edged long sash windows. Set in five acres of landscaped land with splendid views of the ice-encrusted river and the Catskill mountains of the western bank, the house had an air of quiet opulence in keeping with Morton Dyer's position as President and Chairman of Dyer's Business Machines, designers and manufacturers of computers and other business machines.

In the house the day had started quietly once

Morton had left for his office in the D.B.M. factory on the outskirts of the town. It was quiet, that is, until Dandy entered by the kitchen door, crashing into the room, clumping her boots on the mat to clear them of the snow she had walked through on her way from the house of apartments where she lived alone.

'Hi, Marcie,' she called out, a grin curving her generously curved lips and making her deeply set dark brown eyes glint. 'You know where Mom is?'

'Taking her shower, I guess,' replied Marcella, the Dyer's housekeeper. 'What are you doing here this early? Aren't you going to your work?'

'I've got the day off for the wedding rehearsal,' said Dandy. She strode across the gleaming tiles of the kitchen floor leaving dark footprints on the ivory-coloured surface.

'Hey, Dandy, just you take those boots off,' Marcella yelled. 'Leave them by the door. Don't you ever listen to me? You're gonna make a mess on the new carpets and then your Mom is gonna be mad at you.'

But Dandy was already in the wide hallway and making for the graceful curving staircase with its black wrought iron railings and fluffy ivory-coloured carpet. She went up the stairs two at a time moving with the grace of an athlete whose body is in good physical condition; moving more like a boy than a woman of twenty-one and bursting into the master bedroom without stopping to knock on the door.

The room was softly feminine, frilly and sweetly scented, expressive of the woman who had designed the decor. A Mozart *divertimento*, played by a well-known orchestra, issued from a cassette tape recorder built in to the bookcase. Before an antique heart-shaped dressing table set between the two long windows Anne Dyer was sitting. Dressed only in a robe of thin Chinese silk she was leaning forward and examining her finely chiselled, white-skinned face and short, curly red-gold hair in the gilt edged mirror.

'Mom, can I borrow your car?' asked Dandy abruptly.

'Why?' asked Anne coolly. 'What's wrong with yours?'

'The damn . . . *oops*, sorry. I know you don't like me to swear.' Dandy's mischievous grin flashed briefly. 'The starter won't work. And I had it fixed only the other day.' The grin widened into a smile, like a gleam of sunlight in her golden brown face; a smile that possessed a warm melting charm she didn't know about. 'I just need it for a couple of hours to go into Albany. I have some shopping to do.'

'Oh, all right,' Anne said with a sigh. She opened one of the drawers in the dressing table and took out a brown leather handbag from which she took a ring on which there were two keys. She held the keys out to Dandy. 'But don't be too long,' she added. 'Remember the rehearsal starts at noon at the church.'

Dandy took the keys and went over to one of the windows. Although it wasn't snowing, heavy grey clouds were rolling down over the distant mountains and hovering above the river, threatening more snow. Tomorrow's wedding could be white in more ways than one, she thought with a wry grin.

'I know I should have said this before, Mom,'

she said, turning away from the window to look at Anne again, 'but do we really have to have a rehearsal? Somehow a rehearsal seems to take all the fun out of getting married. It makes the whole performance less spontaneous and natural.'

'A wedding isn't a performance,' Anne objected, beginning to smooth make-up on her face.

'I think it is.' Dandy's eyes began to sparkle with the light of battle. 'The way you and Jon's mother have planned it it's a show, a sort of parade, that we'll all dress up for. It doesn't seem to have anything to do with Jon or with the way we feel.'

'Now listen to me, Dandy,' said Anne sharply, swinging round on her stool to face her daughter. 'We're having the rehearsal first of all to please Morton. After all he is paying for everything; for the flowers, the organist and choir, for the dinner and reception and the clothes you and I will wear. Then it's also to please the Reverend Costain. He wants everything to go smoothly and wants the rehearsal so that any mistakes we make can be corrected.' Anne frowned and her glance swept critically over Dandy. 'I hope you're not going to attend in those clothes. In that thick shirt, those pants and those boots you look like a lumberjack.'

Dandy looked down at herself and then at her mother, teasing humour glinting in her dark eyes.

'Perhaps I am a lumberjack at heart,' she replied. 'Perhaps I'm really a man living inside a woman's body.'

'Dandy!' Anne's face wore an expression of horrified disgust. 'I wish you wouldn't talk like that.'

'Why shouldn't I? It's common knowledge there

are such people in the world. Time you faced up to reality, Mom.'

'But you are not one of those people,' said Anne angrily, her greenish eyes flashing. 'You've always been a tomboy but you're entirely female and I still have hopes that once you're married to Jon you'll discard those boyish ways and become more feminine in your behaviour.' She paused, her expression softening. 'You can look very beautiful when you want to,' she continued. 'You have a good figure and when your hair is arranged properly you look as attractive as any magazine cover-girl. You look especially lovely in your bridal gown. Ivory is an excellent colour for you to wear.'

'Why thank you, *Mama mia*,' replied Dandy making a mock curtsey. 'Compliments from you aren't exactly frequent.' Her smile didn't last long. A heavy frown took its place. 'But I still can't help wishing. . . .'

She broke off with a sigh. What point could there be in telling Anne that she wished the arrangements for the wedding weren't so cut and dried; that she wished Jon Van Fleet, the man she was engaged to marry, was different, not so boyish. How she wished he was older, more experienced, more determined and capable of sweeping her off her feet.

She began to smile again. Now she was being silly and thinking like her close friend Sallyanne Porter. Sallyanne was always reading romance novels in which the mysterious, arrogant hero fell in love with the shy, innocent heroine and carried her off to live in his castle in Scotland, or to his sheep station in Australia or to the Greek island he owned.

'You wish what?' Anne prompted gently.

'Oh, I just wish Grandpa Kerr could be at the wedding tomorrow,' muttered Dandy. 'I miss him and it won't seem right without him, somehow.' She gave her mother an underbrowed glance. 'Couldn't we postpone the wedding until May or June, until Gramps is back in this country?'

'Oh, Dandy, we've gone through all this before,' groaned Anne. 'And you agreed to set the date for tomorrow. You know it's to fit in with Jon's work. He has to take his Spring vacation now, the last week in March and the first week in April. We can't change the date of the wedding now. It's too late. Everything is arranged and guests have already arrived from far away.'

Dandy spread her left hand before her and frowned at the engagement ring Jon had given her. The small diamond glittered coldly. She hated it and hadn't wanted to wear it. Her independent nature rejected it, seeing in it, as well as in a wedding ring, the shackle of slavery.

'I wish I hadn't agreed to marry Jon,' she said suddenly. 'I'm only getting married to him to please you and Morton, you know.'

'But you like Jon,' exclaimed Anne. 'You've said you do. And he likes you. You've been friends for years.'

'I like Jon,' Dandy said, in agreement. 'But I don't feel passionate about him. I don't feel anything here.' She thumped her left breast with a fist. 'He doesn't turn me on.'

'What a way to talk,' Anne said with a touch of derision. 'Passion isn't for real. It happens only in books. I suppose you've been reading some of those romances Sallyanne always has her nose in.

They aren't at all true to life, you know. They're just fantasies.'

'Who wants to read anything that's true to life?' retorted Dandy. 'Anything that is true to life is dull and boring. What's so wonderful about our way of life here that anyone would want to read about it? Nothing ever happens that's exciting. Every day is the same. Only the seasons change.' She gave Anne another curious glance. 'Are you sure it exists only in books, passion with a capital P, I mean? Didn't you feel passionate about my father?'

As she had expected Anne avoided replying to the question and swung round on the dressing stool to face the mirror again. Picking up a lipstick she began to smooth colour over her lips.

'While you're in Albany you might call in to see Cora and make sure she knows about delivering the bouquet to this house early tomorrow morning with the posies for the bridesmaids and the corsage for me and the *boutonnière* for Morton,' Anne said coolly.

'You won't talk about him, ever,' retorted Dandy scornfully. 'You've never talked to me about him. Why not? Why won't you talk to me about my own father? I have a right to know about him, to know what he was like as a man. What did he do to you that you won't talk about him to me?'

'He died, that's what he did,' Anne retorted, roused at last, her voice edged with bitterness. 'He got himself killed. He would go off on that mountaineering expedition to Everest when I was expecting you.' She drew in a ragged breath. 'I pleaded with him not to go, but climbing that mountain was more important to him than I was. So now you know. You know why I won't talk about him. He got himself killed and . . . and left me all alone.'

'It was an accident,' said Dandy quietly. 'He didn't get himself killed deliberately. He didn't know he was going to be caught in an avalanche.'

'But he didn't have to go,' argued Anne. 'He could have stayed with me until you were born. He was reckless, always taking chances.'

'He liked to live, to get the most out of life,' replied Dandy defensively. 'Gramps has told me that. And you loved him, you were passionately in love with him. You must have been or you wouldn't have lived with him before you were married to him. That's why you won't talk about him. You don't want to admit that you loved him passionately and . . .'

'That's enough. You've said too much,' Anne ordered, but her voice was choked and tears were slipping down her cheeks. Anne always so cool, so elegant was actually weeping.

'Oh, Mom, I'm sorry,' Dandy muttered, her generous heart touched by her mother's distress. 'I didn't mean to hurt you I've never meant to hurt you but I guess I always have because I don't behave the way you'd like me to behave. But I have been trying this past year or so. I really have.'

'I know. I know,' whispered Anne. She sniffed and taking a tissue from a box dabbed at her eyes and cheeks. 'And I hope you'll be happy with Jon. Passionate love isn't always the best sort of love,' she went on, making an effort to pass on some experience to her wilful yet loveable daughter. 'It

often flares up between two people who are
entirely unsuited to each other and who find, after
a while, they can't live together. It seems to me
that people who are not passionately in love often
make the best marriages. They learn to love each
other over a period of time.'

'Like you and Morton have?'

'Yes, yes,' said Anne quickly. 'Like Morton and
me.'

'I see,' Dandy sighed. 'But that isn't the sort of
relationship I want with a man. I had a terrible
night last night. I couldn't sleep for thinking that I
don't want to marry Jon. I don't. I don't.'

'Oh, everyone has nights like that before getting
married,' said Anne lightly. 'You'll feel much
better after we've done the rehearsal and once
you're dressed up tomorrow and on your way to
church you'll stop feeling nervous. The cold-feet
feeling will go.'

'But you don't seem to understand. I don't want
to marry Jon because I feel we won't stay
together,' argued Dandy. 'You see I've found out
that he's been seeing someone else.'

'You mean he's been dating another woman?'
Anne swung round again on the stool.

'Right.'

'How long have you known?'

'About a month.'

'Then why have you let us fix the date and make
all the arrangements?' demanded Anne. She was
angry again.

'I don't know. I don't know,' cried Dandy,
beating her thighs with her fists as she strode
about the room. 'Oh, what am I going to do? I
don't want to marry a boy I've known all my life. I

want someone older, with more experience and . . .'

'Stop it,' Anne ordered sternly. 'You've given your word to Jon and if you break it now, if you jilt him, you'll be the talk of Renwick. I can't allow you to do that to Jon, to his parents or to Morton and me.' She saw rebellion flaring in Dandy's face and that sense of inadequacy which always came over her when she was trying to cope with her daughter swept through her. She was taking the wrong attitude as usual. Softening a little, she leaned towards Dandy. 'Jon is very fond of you and I think he needs you,' she said.

'Does he?' Dandy's lips curled sardonically. 'The problem is I don't need him. I never did and I never will.' She turned towards the bedroom door. 'I'm off, now, to Albany. But don't forget, Mom, whatever happens I'll always love you.'

'Happens? What is going to happen?' exclaimed Anne.

'I don't know yet,' replied Dandy with a grin. 'But Gramps is always saying that nothing ever does happen unless you make it happen and that's the way life should be lived. See you later.'

'Dandy. Wait!' Anne sprang to her feet. 'Come back!'

But Dandy had gone, going down the stairs two at a time the way she had come up them, her mane of brown-black hair flying out behind her. Through the kitchen she whirled like a tornado and out through the door, banging it behind her so that Marcella winced and rolled her eyes.

Nearly two hours later, her last-minute shopping done, Dandy left Albany and, turning her back on the slender grey towers of the State Plaza, drove towards the complicated interchange of roads which lead in all directions from the New York State capital city; a maze of criss-crossing routes designed to confuse strangers. With the casual ease of someone who had lived all her life in the area, Dandy chose unerringly the road that would take her over the bridge that crossed the river, to the east bank. It was eleven-thirty and snow was beginning to fall, flurries of small flakes that cut down visibility and made the surface of roads slippery.

In half an hour she ought to be at the Episcopal Church of St Agnes, the church where her mother had been married to her stepfather and where all the Dyer family had been married for generations.

'But I'm not a Dyer,' Dandy muttered to the windshield. 'I'm a Kerr and a bit of a rebel and I'm not going to that wedding rehearsal. I'm not going. I'm not going. Oh, Gramps I wish you were here to give me some advice. What shall I do? I know I've only myself to blame for this mess I'm in. But what shall I do to get out of it? I don't want to marry Jon.'

If only her grandfather hadn't gone away last November on one of his fact-finding missions for another novel. He wrote political thrillers using his experience as a one-time member of the Central Intelligence Agency and had twice hit the number one spot on the New York best-sellers list. She had wanted to go with him when he had left New York last autumn, had pleaded with him to take her with him, but he had refused.

'It wouldn't work,' he had said. 'I like to go at my own speed and that wouldn't be yours. You've got to get on with your own life and have your own adventures.'

'I'll miss you,' she had replied. 'I always do. You're the only person who understands me. Supposing I do something awful while you're away, what shall I do without you to run to?'

It had been then that he had pressed a key into her hand and had whispered, 'It's the key to the padlock on the cabin in Vermont, just in case the going gets tough and you want to hole up somewhere.'

Remembering that conversation now Dandy slid her hand into the pocket of her thick woollen, shirt-like jacket. Her fingers closed around her worn ring of keys. She had the key to the cabin that her grandfather had built in Vermont with the help of her own father when he had been alive. She could go to the cabin now if she wanted. All she had to do was to continue along this road until she reached Interstate Highway 91 coming up from Massachusetts and take the highway north to St Johnsbury in Vermont. From that town it wasn't far along a country road to a small lake called Kerr's Pond where the cabin was located.

The exit road to Renwick loomed on the right. In the distance she could see the white spire of St Agnes's Church gleaming among the dark tracery of winter-bare elm trees. She looked back at the road before her. Instead of slowing down and moving over into the right lane to take the exit she put her foot down on the accelerator. The car leapt forward, its tyres swishing on the wet tarmac.

'Thanks Gramps,' she whispered to her absent grandfather, as if he were there in the car beside her. 'I knew you'd come through.'

It wasn't the first time she had run away. There had been that time she had run away from the girl's private school in Connecticut. She had been thirteen years old, an ugly duckling with braces on her teeth making smiling forbidden and with lowering black eyebrows giving her face a perpetually stormy expression.

She had been sent to the school by her stepfather mostly to get her out of his house and away from her mother. Anne had agreed to let her attend the school in desperation, hoping that a few years in the school would change her tomboyish daughter into a well-educated socialite.

Dandy had been very unhappy at the school. Cut off from the two people she had loved most, her mother and her grandfather, she had been in trouble with the teachers and the other girls from the first day. She had been at the school only two months when she had decided to run away. She had gone by bus as far north as she could and then had hitched lifts to her grandfather's cabin nestling beside the lake among the tree-covered hills of north-eastern Vermont. He had understood how she had felt about the school and had intervened on her behalf with her stepfather. She had not been sent back to the school but had attended public schools, until she had reached the age of eighteen.

The ugly duckling of thirteen had developed into a graceful athlete, good at most sports and, though she had turned out to be not actually brilliant at mathematics, she had been bright enough to train at D.B.M. as a computer programmer, where she still worked and would continue to work after she had married Jon.

If she married Jon. She frowned as she peered through the windshield at the wet grey surface of the road. Why the hell had she accepted his proposal? He had proposed at a Christmas Eve party given by his parents in the ultra-contemporary house not far from the Dyer house.

She must have been drunk on too much egg nog at the time and, come to think of it now, Jon hadn't been particularly sober either. Maybe if Gramps had been home for Christmas she wouldn't have let herself be persuaded that marriage to Jon was a good idea, and she wouldn't be running away now.

A green signpost appeared. It indicated that the next exit would take her on to the Highway going north. It was now or never. She could turn back and go to the rehearsal or drive north. The car slowed down and she guided it round the curve of a service road, under an overpass and on to the three-laned highway where container trucks and other vehicles were speeding by.

Her foot pressed down on the accelerator again and the car rolled forward into the right-hand lane. She was on her way north, on the road again and doing something she loved to do—driving a fast car along a fast road. Her spirits lifted, she flicked on the radio, turning to a country and western channel, and for the next eighty or so miles she sang along with Dolly Parton, Loretta Lynn, Willie Nelson and Kenny Rogers and other favourites, never once thinking of Jon or the wedding rehearsal she should have attended that day.

By the time she reached the exit for St Johnsbury the weather was deteriorating and the afternoon light was dim. Snow was falling thickly and electric lights were twinkling in the small town. She pulled into the first gas station she came to and, while the pump attendant was filling the tank of the car, she hurried into the small restaurant to use the phone. She called her mother's number collect and in a few moments heard Anne accepting the charges. Anne's voice sharpened as she said,

'Dandy? At last, thank God. Where are you? What's happened?'

'I'm not going to tell you where I am,' said Dandy, ignoring her mother's attempts to interrupt her. 'I've just called to let you know I'm all right.'

'I've been worried sick about you,' said Anne, her usually toneless voice roughened by anxiety. 'To say nothing about my car. Morton and Jon are out searching Albany for you and Morton has reported you as missing to the police. He thought that someone might have kidnapped you. Dandy, you haven't been kidnapped, have you?'

'No, I haven't. I'm all right. I've told you.'

'Then come right back home.'

'No. Mother, please listen to me. I'm not coming back tonight.'

'But you must. You're going to be married tomorrow.'

'No, I'm not. Not tomorrow. Please tell Jon I'm sorry but I can't go through with it tomorrow. I must have more time to think. I must be by myself for a while.'

'You can't do this.' Anne was almost shouting. 'You can't run away any more. You're not a kid. You must start taking responsibility. . . .'

'I am. That's just what I'm doing, taking responsibility for my own actions, my own life.'

'But everything is arranged for tomorrow.

You're letting everyone down by running away, don't you see that?' argued Anne. 'Dandy, you've got to come home tonight.'

'I'm sorry, Mom. I can't. I'm sorry to cause you trouble but I made a mistake when I agreed to marry Jon. Look, I have to go now. I'll call you again on Sunday to tell you what I'm going to do.'

She hung up quickly and stepped out of the phone booth into the steaminess of the restaurant. At the counter she ordered a hamburger and a coffee to take out to the car with her. The pump attendant was wiping the mud and dirt off the windshield of the car.

'Looks like we're in for another big storm tonight,' he said cheerfully. 'Last one of the winter, I hope. Great for the ski-ing folks, though. Where you heading for?'

'Greenbury,' she said vaguely.

'You'd best get a move on, then. They say those country roads are closing up pretty fast with snow.'

Leaving St Johnsbury and the highway behind her Dandy drove along a winding country road towards the village of Greenbury. Fortunately there was a tractor with a snow-plough in front of her most of the way, pushing the snow to the side of the road and an hour later she was driving down into a hollow between the hills, where lights glittered from the windows on a cluster of houses.

Once she was through the village she turned off the road on to a lane that wound along the valley of a small river to Kerr's Pond. The lane hadn't been ploughed. Thick drifts of snow clogged it so she couldn't see the edges of the road and often found herself driving perilously close to the ice-covered river.

The grey veil of snowflakes whirling perpetually towards the windshield had a curious mesmeric effect on her and she could see only a few feet in front of the car. After sliding and bumping along for a few miles she decided to give up the unequal struggle when the car plunged into a deep drift and refused to go either backwards or forwards.

She turned off the car lights, got out of the car and locked the doors. Fastening her jacket to the neck and turning up its collar she began to walk, her shoulder bag slung over one shoulder, her hands deep in her pockets, one of them clenched around her ring of keys. As she floundered through heaps of soft snow her fingers searched for and found the small round-headed key which would open the padlock on the hasp of the log cabin's door. It was her one link with her grandfather. It was her talisman capable of working wonders and changing her life. It was like the lamp Aladdin had found. She rubbed it between finger and thumb.

'Bring me luck,' she whispered. 'Oh, bring me luck. You've no idea how much I could do with a little luck right now.'

After about half an hour of blundering through the snow she decided she must be near the cabin. Darkness had come early, increasing the difficulty of seeing anything through the veil of flakes. She was almost covered from head to foot in snow, having slipped and fallen several times, her eyes were watering from the sting of the icy wind and she was beginning to ache. Pausing for a moment she pushed back her wet hair and looked around, hoping to see the cabin.

A yellow light twinkled. It was surely coming from a window. And wasn't that the shape of a building she could see among a cluster of trees? She began to push through the snow again. The thick soft stuff was almost waist high and she wished she was wearing snowshoes or even skis.

The yellow light flickered. She was quite near to it now and could see the shape of the small barn beside the house where the electrical generator was located. Since there was a light in the cabin someone must be in it. Who? Had someone broken in? Perhaps a hobo was living in it for the winter. Gramps had told her that sometimes vagrants did break into country cabins during the bad weather and stayed in them, clearing out when the thaw came and before the owners arrived to make the places ready for the summer.

Suddenly the light went out. She blinked. Snow swirled around her. The wind nipped her cheeks. She could see the path to the cabin now. Someone had dug it out after last night's snow but the clearing was fast disappearing under fresh drifts of snow. She started to walk up the path, sniffing as she went. Was that woodsmoke she could smell?

Hope danced through her. Perhaps Gramps had come back from his travels without letting her mother or her know. He did that sometimes when he wanted to be alone to write a new book.

She hurried towards the door. Her fingers groped for the padlock. It wasn't there. She didn't need her key after all. Cautiously she lifted the latch, every sense on the alert because whoever was in the house might resent her intrusion and challenge her. The hinges of the door creaked loudly as she pushed it open. She stepped inside and tried to pierce the darkness. The smell of woodsmoke was very strong and she could see firelight glowing in the old Franklin stove, orange light showing around the edges of the closed doors.

She shut the cabin door and stood listening. Water dripped down her face from her hair and from her clothing to the wooden floor. Logs crackled in the stove. Wind moaned in the chimney. Snowflakes pattered stealthily against the window panes. She took a step forward and stopped to listen again. Was that someone breathing? The hair at the back of her neck prickled. She took another step forward.

'Don't move.' The voice that spoke out of the darkness just to the right of her was cool, crisp and very masculine, but it wasn't her grandfather's voice. 'Stay right there and tell me who you are and what you want,' the voice ordered.

Dandy didn't stop to think. Taking hold of her shoulder bag she flung it in the direction of the voice and pivoting on her left foot brought her right leg and foot up in a heel kick, aiming to strike anywhere on the dark figure she could just see in the darkness.

But her foot never touched him because he blocked the kick with an arm, caught her foot in his other hand and threw her down on to her back. She fell with a crash, all the breath knocked out of her, every bone and muscle in her body jarred. She was on her feet in a flash, knowing that he had moved behind her. Pivoting again she brought her right leg and foot up in a roundhouse kick. This time her foot connected with his chest. He grunted and went staggering back against the cabin wall.

She waited breathing hard, trying to see where he was and trying to remember where the light switch was. It was on the wall by the door. She stepped sideways angling towards the door, her arm reaching out, her fingers feeling along the rough logs and finding a switch. She felt it. To her surprise it was in the ON position. She flicked it. No light came on.

'What's happened to the lights?' she exclaimed.

There was no reply. Where was he? She whirled around and aimed another kick but her foot had hardly left the ground when he charged at her. His arms went around her. Long, lean and hard they held her like a vice. She brought her knee up into his groin and heard him grunt with pain but his arms didn't slacken. They held her tighter and tighter until she could feel the thrust of his hips against hers and her breasts were crushed by his chest. She felt as if her bones would crack under the pressure and she was finding it hard to breathe, but she could still use her knee and she did, viciously.

This time he didn't just grunt. He exclaimed in a foreign language then growled in English,

'Bitch. There's only one way to deal with you.'

His hard fingers gripped her chin. His nails scraped her skin. She opened her mouth to cry out but her cry was smothered by his lips which came down hard on hers in a brutal silencing kiss.

Fury shot like fire through Dandy. She tried to break free from his cruel embrace but there wasn't any way she could make the iron bands of his arms relax and his lips seemed to be glued to hers.

She decided to go limp and fall backwards, hoping he would release her when he felt himself falling with her. Her plan succeeded too well. She lost her balance and fell backwards, but he stayed with her all the way until he was on top of her, pinning her to the floor with his weight, his mouth dominating hers. She couldn't move and she could hardly breath and slowly panic began to spread through her. Frantically she kicked out and tried to twist from beneath him, but the more she struggled the harder he pressed against her.

She stopped twisting and closed her eyes, hoping to deceive him into thinking she had fainted. The hard pressure of his lips relaxed slightly but his lips didn't leave hers. Instead, they began to move sensually as if he found the taste and feel of her lips to his liking. Then the warm moist tip of his tongue flickered along the line of her lips and she opened her eyes quickly in alarm as she felt, deep within her, a response to that suggestive caress.

Again she tried to twist free without success. One of his hands slid under her jacket then under her sweater. Warm to her chilled skin his fingertips stroked upwards and suddenly, amazingly there was no resistance left in her. Her lips parted uncontrollably and her tongue flickered out to meet his. New, mind-dizzying sensations tingled through her threatening to overcome all sensible thought. She experienced another sharp dagger-thrust of alarm and finding her hands free she began to beat at his shoulders and then to push at them with all her strength.

At that moment the electric light flickered and came on, flooding the room with brightness. The man lifted his head, rolled away from her, stood up and walked out of her sight.

CHAPTER TWO

DANDY sat up. She felt bruised and battered but she accepted the feeling as part of the battle that had just taken place between her and the man. But she also felt violated by the way he had kissed her and had touched her and that made her angry. The karate she had learned in the past six months, ever since she had started attending a course in martial arts at the D.B.M. gymnasium, hadn't helped her at all because she had come up against an opponent who was much stronger than she was; someone who was as lithe and as swift as a panther; someone who didn't keep to the rules of karate and had used other methods of assault and had dominated her with his lips and tongue, defeating her by touching her in a sensual, suggestive way. For doing that he would have to pay. She would get her revenge somehow.

She wiped her hand across her throbbing lips and turned to look at him, glowering through the twin black curtains of her parted hair which had fallen forward over her face. She was afraid of what she might see. She was afraid she had been kissed and touched by someone who was dirty, vile and repulsive and she couldn't contain a shudder of disgust.

He was standing by the table in the karate Heiko-tachi stance, his feet apart at about shoulder width with the toes straight in front of him, his arms held slightly in front of his body, the

26

hands clenched into fists. He was ready to defend or attack. She rolled over and stood up in a quick lithe movement so she could face him. Shaking her hair back from her face she also took up the Heiko-tachi stance. They eyed each other warily.

He was about six feet tall and was compactly built with straight flat shoulders and a wide chest tapering to a lean waist and hips and muscular thighs that shaped his black corduroy pants. The hair coiling about his forehead was blue-black, quite a different darkness from hers and it contrasted strongly with the creamy white pallor of his face. His features were perfectly chiselled, the forehead high, the nose aquiline, the chin rounded yet strong, the lips firm yet generously curved and his eyes were blue-grey, very clear, startlingly light between thick black lashes and set beneath slanting finely drawn black eyebrows.

He wasn't vile or repulsive. He wasn't dirty or ragged. He was handsome and his clothes were of good quality, the corduroy of his pants as smooth as velvet, the high-necked woollen sweater he was wearing the same colour as his eyes. But he wasn't wearing shoes or boots, only thick grey socks. No wonder she hadn't heard him moving.

'Who are you and what are you doing in my grandfather's cabin?' she demanded glaring at him from under scowling eyebrows, taking the offensive as usual, always believing in attack being the best form of defence.

His eyebrows went up in surprise and his clear glance swept over her from head to foot. He laughed shortly and jeeringly. Irritated by his mockery Dandy gritted her teeth and her hands clenched at her sides.

'I don't believe it,' he said and laughed again, shaking his head from side to side. 'I don't believe that you are the granddaughter of the famous Douglas Kerr. You look like a hippy.' His glance raked her again. 'And you're dressed like a tramp,' he added scornfully.

'Snob, patronising snob,' she hissed at him furiously. She had friends who were hippies and a few years ago when she had been eighteen she had joined them to live for a while in a commune on an island off the coast of Maine. Admittedly her stay with them hadn't lasted more than a summer because she had got fed up with being hungry and had also quarrelled with the leader of the group, a man called Gerry who had wanted her to be his lover. But even though she had left the group to return to Renwick and had gone to work at D.B.M. she was still inclined to the hippy philosophy of life, believing in naturalness in all things, and that was why she didn't use make-up and was careless about the way she dressed.

She dug her hand into her jacket pocket and brought out her ring of keys. She held up the key which opened the padlock of the cabin door.

'Look at that,' she said advancing towards him. 'It's the key to this place. If you'd like to find the padlock I'll show you how it fits.' He stared at the key and she added as scornfully as she could, 'But I guess you smashed the padlock when you broke in and entered the cabin.'

At that moment the electric light flickered and went out, plunging the room into darkness again.

'Oh, what happened?' exclaimed Dandy.

'Power failure,' he replied coolly. 'It happened just before you walked in, too. Something is wrong

with the generator. Where are you going?' His
voice rasped harshly as he questioned her and she
collided with him as she stepped forward. It was
like colliding with a rock and she stepped back
quickly, afraid he might maul her again.

'I'm going to the stove to open its door so that
the fire will give us some light,' she retorted
practically. 'Then I'm going to find a flashlight
and I'm going down into the basement to look for
the oil lamps and kerosene that Gramps always
keeps down there for when the power fails. And
that should prove to you once and for all that I am
related to Douglas Kerr and have a right to be in
this cabin.'

He didn't argue with her but stepped aside. She
walked over to the stove. On top of it she found
the curved steel handle for opening the doors. She
slipped one end through an iron ring on one of the
doors and pulled the door open. Then she opened
the other door. Firelight, hot and orange-coloured,
blazed forth, lighting up the log walls, the old
chairs and table, glinting on the china and glass on
the dresser and burnishing the face of the man
who had followed her across the room.

Dandy reached behind the stove for the
firescreen. When it was in place she went over to
the dresser and opened one of the drawers.
Reaching in she took out a big black-covered
flashlight. The man snatched it from her and she
turned on him. They glared at each other
belligerently.

'I'll hold it,' he said.

'Why?' she challenged. 'Are you afraid I might
hit you with it?'

'Right.' His lips relaxed into a faint smile.

'There is a potential for violence in you that I don't trust. You seem to be capable of hitting me on the back of the head with it when my back is turned.'

'You think I'm violent?' she exclaimed. 'What about you? You threw me to the floor. I'm bruised all over.'

'You only got what was coming to you,' he retorted. 'You attacked first and without warning.'

'I attacked in self-defence,' she retaliated angrily. 'I could hear you creeping up on me. For all I knew you were going to pounce on me. And you're the intruder here. I'm not. I belong here and now I'm going to the basement to find Gramp's survival kit. But I can only go down with the flashlight, so give it back to me.'

'No. I'll shine it for you,' he replied. 'How do we get down to the basement?'

'Through the trap door. Over here.'

She walked over to a corner of the room on the left side of the doorway and kicked aside a rag rug. Bending down she found the brass ring set into one of the floorboards. While the man shone the flashlight she tugged at the ring. A wide trap door lifted up. The beam of the flashlight shone down into the opening, revealing a wooden ladder.

Dandy went down the ladder, realising too late that he could close the trap door on her and imprison her in the basement if he wanted to. Much to her relief when she reached the bottom of the ladder he came down it after her.

'So where is the survival kit you talk about?' he demanded shining the flashlight around the basement walls. 'Doug didn't tell me about it.'

'It's here, in this cupboard built into the wall.'

She pulled open the cupboard door. 'Do you have any idea what's wrong with the generator?'

'Probably the spark plugs of the engine need cleaning or replacing,' he replied. 'I'll examine it if I can get to the shed through the snow.'

The shelves of the cupboard were loaded with all sorts of canned food and on the bottom shelf there were two oil lamps with tall glass chimneys, a two-burner kerosene cooking stove and a two-gallon can of kerosene. There was also a waterproof bag containing matches.

They took everything they needed up the ladder and closed the trap door. At the table Dandy poured oil into the lamps and lit the wicks. When both wicks were burning steadily she placed the glass chimneys over them. Soft yellow light shone out across the table revealing a loaf of French bread, a plate of smoked meats, big hunk of Vermont cheese and a bowl of apples and oranges.

'Gosh, I'm hungry,' gasped Dandy, forgetting her antipathy to the strange man. She sat on one of the chairs. 'Would you mind if I had some bread and meat?'

'Help yourself,' he said. 'I'd just made coffee when the light went out. Would you like some?'

'Please.' Dandy seized the bread knife and sawed off a thick slice of the loaf, spread butter on it, placed a piece of cheese and one of meat on it and began to eat ravenously. She had almost finished eating the open sandwich when the man returned from the kitchen area of the room with a coffee pot and two mugs. He sat down opposite her, poured the coffee and then made a sandwich for himself.

Dandy gulped down hot coffee, helped herself to

more bread, meat and cheese. From under her eyelashes she studied the man while she ate. For all the notice he took of her she might not have been in the room and for some reason it annoyed her to think he was deliberately ignoring her.

'I think it's time you told me who you are and what you're doing here,' she said bluntly.

He gave her a cold glance and standing up went over to the dresser. He took something from the top of the dresser, came back to the table and dropped the something in front of her on to the table. Hard and heavy, it thudded. It was the padlock from the door of the cabin and it hadn't been damaged.

'I opened it with this,' he said and produced a key that was the exact replica of the key on her ring. 'Doug gave it to me before he went away last November,' said the man. 'He told me I could come here any time I wished, especially if I wanted to be alone. I felt a need to be alone this weekend so I came yesterday.'

'A place to hole up in, would be what he said,' Dandy murmured. 'He said the same to me.' She leaned towards him. 'Do you believe now that I'm his granddaughter?'

'Do you believe now that I didn't break into this cabin?' he retorted.

'Yes, I believe you, now that I've seen the key.' She smiled suddenly, that smile of melting warmth that changed her face and gave it a fleeting beauty and held out her hand to him across the table. 'I'm Dandy Kerr Dyer, actually my given names are Doris Amanda but Gramps has always called me Dandy, thank goodness. And I'm sorry I kicked you. You see I was anxious when I saw a light in the cabin and when it went out so suddenly, I really thought someone had broken in and was waiting in the darkness to attack me.'

After a brief hesitation he took hold of her hand and shook it. His grip was strong, but his hand didn't linger in hers. He poured more coffee for himself and began to drink it.

'You're supposed to tell me your name now,' she said bluntly.

'You can call me Yvan,' he replied with a shrug.

'Well, that's a new one on me. Sounds sort of Russian,' she remarked. 'Are you from Russia?'

'No.' He was curt and shook his head and then asked a question as if to stop her from throwing another question at him. 'Where did you learn karate?'

'So you recognised my kicks.' She was pleased that they had been recognisable. 'Gramps once showed me a few moves. He said it's important for a woman to know how to defend herself against assault these days when there's so much violence about. So I've been attending a course in martial arts at the company sports club. I haven't got a black belt yet, but the instuctor says I'm pretty good.'

'You are,' he agreed. 'And at first I thought you were a young man.'

'Lots of other people have told me that,' she sighed. 'I guess it's because I'm tall and lean. But I didn't stand a chance against you. You must work out every day to be in such great physical condition.' She spoke admiringly, hoping to draw him out, but he didn't rise to the bait. Remaining silent he drained the coffee in the pot into his mug.

Irritated by his cool reserved manner Dandy blurted, 'But you broke the rules by kissing me.'

'Did I? I wasn't aware that there are any rules when it comes to defending oneself,' he retorted.

'Why did you kiss me?'

'As soon as I found out you were a woman I knew I had to find some way of defeating you without hitting you,' he replied. 'I had to do something. That second kick of yours landed where it hurts ... badly. And so did your knee.' His lips curved in a slight smile. 'And then I much prefer to kiss a woman than to hit her,' he added softly. 'What do you prefer? To be hit? Or to be kissed?'

The clear blue-grey eyes smiled directly into hers and to her own secret amazement her cheeks flamed with colour. Avoiding his gaze she looked down at the table.

'I prefer to be treated as an equal,' she muttered stiffly.

'Oh, surely not,' he scoffed. 'Surely you prefer to be treated as someone superior. You wouldn't like me to treat you as I would treat another man, would you?'

Feeling strongly that she would lose any argument about equality between the sexes that she might become involved in with him, she was silent for a few seconds, searching for a way to change the subject. At last she said,

'My grandfather has never told me about you.'

'He has never told me about you either,' he returned. 'I didn't know he has a daughter who also has a daughter.'

'Oh, he doesn't have a daughter. My father was Gramps' only son, Bruce Kerr. He was a photographer and explorer. He was killed on the slopes of Everest. Later my mother married again and my stepfather adopted me. That's why I have his last name as well as Kerr. When and where did you meet Gramps?'

'About two years ago on a ski-trail, near Stowe. He had fallen and had hurt his leg. I stopped and helped him. We kept in touch.'

'Do you live near here?'

'I've been living in Canada for the past seven years.' He glanced at her. 'Your clothes are very wet. They are beginning to steam.'

She glanced down at her damp jacket, sweater and pants. He was right, they were beginning to steam in the warmth of the room.

'I must look a mess,' she muttered, pushing her hair back.

'You do,' he agreed maddeningly. 'Are you going to stay the night?'

'Of course I am. That's why I've come here, to stay for a couple of days. Any objections?' She glowered challengingly at him.

'If I have any objections and make them known to you you'll probably tell me I have no right to object to you being here because you belong here and I don't,' he replied mockingly. 'So I'm not going to object. How did you get here?'

'I drove up but I had to leave my car in a drift. It'll be buried in snow by now and I probably won't be able to get it out until the snow starts to thaw. What about you? How did you get here?'

'I drove here too and my car was buried by last night's snow. I hope it thaws before Monday because I have to be back in Montreal by then.'

'If the snow doesn't stop we could be here

together for days,' said Dandy, and felt a sudden surge of excitement.

'I hope not,' he said with a blunt honesty that put to an end any romantic fantasies she might have indulged in.

'I think I'll get out of these clothes,' she said. 'Which room are you ... have you been sleeping in?'

'The one at the back.' He gestured towards a door behind him.

'Then I'll sleep in Gramps' room,' she said. 'I hope I can find something to wear in there. I forgot to bring a change of clothes with me.'

'I could lend you something, a pair of jeans and a sweater,' he offered politely and she turned to smile at him. Above the soft golden glow of the oil lamp she had picked up to light her way to the bedroom her face shone.

'Thank you. That's kind of you,' she said. 'But I've just remembered that Gramps always leaves some clothes in the blanket chest in his room. I guess I'll find something in there.'

In the front bedroom she opened the cedar chest that was at the foot of the bed. A strong smell of mothballs exuded from it. There were pairs of corduroys and checked working shirts belonging to her grandfather, all of them much too wide and long for her because Douglas Kerr was over six feet tall and weighed two hundred pounds. But she found an old flannel nightgown of her own, one she had worn at Christmas a few years previously when she had stayed at the cabin with Douglas while her mother and Morton had been abroad. She tossed the gown on the bed, closed the chest and began to peel off her damp clothing.

When she was stripped she carried the oil lamp over to the long mirror attached to the clothes closet door. As she had expected she had a big purplish bruise on her right hip which was the result of being thrown to the floor. It was impossible for her to see if she had any bruises on her buttocks or her spine. She leaned closer to the mirror and peered at her lips. Yes, there was a dark blister forming on the fullness of her lower lip.

'Brute, Animal,' she whispered fiercely, but she wasn't calling herself names. In her imagination she was talking to the man in the other room who had deliberately kissed her so as to immobilise her once he had found out she was a woman.

Then she remembered what had happened when she had closed her eyes and had gone limp under him, how his kiss had changed and how his hands had moved over her caressingly. She remembered how she had longed to respond to the need she had sensed in him; a need to make love to a woman; a need to be loved by a woman. His loneliness of spirit had cried out to her silently in the darkness and had touched her vulnerable, generous heart.

She shivered suddenly in the icy air and the lamp rocked in her hand. She put the lamp down and slipped the nightgown over her head. Dark pink in colour, scattered with tiny white flowers it had ruffles at the neckline and at the end of the long sleeves. It was a Granny gown, so called because its design was based on the nightgowns once worn by country women in the Victorian age to keep them warm in bed when there had been no central heating in the wooden houses they had

inhabited in the cold northern States. This gown
had been given to her by Anne five years ago as a
Christmas present.

Since she had last worn it she had grown taller
and her body had matured so that it was a struggle
to push her arms into the sleeves and to pull it
down over her shoulders. The sleeves were too
short, the hem reached only to the calfs of her legs
and the bodice was stretched taut across her full
breasts so that she couldn't do up the buttons of
the long slit fastening and the cleft between her
breasts showed when she moved.

She couldn't help laughing at her appearance as
she braided her hair into a long thick pigtail. The
change in hair style changed her appearance.
Except for the way her breasts seemed to want to
burst the nightgown apart and the length of her
arms and legs, she looked like a teenager, innocent
and just a little prim.

Taking her damp clothing with her she went
back to the living room, glad to leave the arctic
conditions of the bedroom for the more hell-like
warmth of the big comfortable room where the fire
leapt and crackled.

Yvan had cleared the table and had apparently
washed the dishes for they were stacked in a
drainer by the sink. He was sitting at the table and
seemed to be engrossed in reading a book. Dandy
hung her clothes on the backs of two chairs near
to the stove and then looked back at Yvan.

He was staring at her bare feet. Slowly his
glance lifted, considered her legs for a moment
before moving up to linger provocatively on the
unbuttoned opening of the nightgown.

'What is that you're wearing?' he asked.

'An old nightgown of mine.' She lifted the skirt of the gown to show her knees and a good part of her thighs and did a little dance step. 'Sexy, isn't it?' she remarked daringly.

'That is not the word I would use to describe it,' he replied dampeningly and turned back to his book, leaning both elbows on the table and cupping his chin in his hands, ignoring her again, showing her that he wished she wasn't there.

Dandy dragged a big rocking chair nearer to the stove and sat down. She hunched up her knees and put her bare feet on the seat, pulling down the skirt of the nightgown as far as it would go. Linking her arms about her knees she rocked back and forth, watching Yvan from under her lashes.

Yvan what? Or what Yvan? She didn't know whether the name he had given her was his first name or his family name. Questions bubbled up inside her wanting to be asked. Never had she felt so curious about a man and never had she stared at one for so long, she rebuked herself, and dragged her gaze away from his profile to look at the red heart of the fire instead.

Her eyes narrowed and her lips thinned. She still had to be revenged on him for that kiss. What could she do to punish him? Her lips lost their tight line and curved in a mischievous grin. If only she could lead him on, tempt him to kiss her again and then repulse him. That would be revenge.

She began to sing softly to herself, the tone of her voice rich and natural. She sang the first two verses of one of her favourite contemporary folk songs, Pete Seeger's lament for the young men killed in war, *Where Have All the Flowers Gone*. All the time she was singing she watched the man

at the table until she was sure he wasn't reading
but was listening to the song. Then she sang a
simple little love song by the Canadian troubadour
Leonard Cohen, repeating the last four lines twice,
wishing she had her guitar with her so that she
could accompany herself.

> *'And how I kissed you then*
> *and you kissed me*
> *shy as though I'd*
> *never been your lover.'*

The deep soft cadence of her voice seemed to
linger hauntingly in the silence of the room after she
had finished singing but Yvan didn't look up and he
made no comment. Yet she knew he had been
touched by the song because his eyebrows slanted
together in a frown and instead of cupping his chin
his hands were clenched at his temples, the whiteness
of bone showing through the tanned skin.

'Are you married?' Dandy asked. It was a while
before he replied.

'No.' He spoke curtly.

'Neither am I. But I'm supposed to be getting
married tomorrow morning at eleven o'clock in
Renwick, the town where I live.'

'I had noticed the engagement ring.' His voice
was dry.

She unclasped her hands and held her left one
up in front of her, staring at it in surprise. She had
forgotten about the ring.

'Pretty, isn't it?' she remarked mockingly. 'But it
doesn't mean a thing.'

He looked at her sharply. From under the black
eyebrows his pale eyes glittered as hard and cold
as the diamond on her finger.

'It probably means something to the guy who bought it,' he rebuked her. 'It probably set him back a few hundred bucks.'

'Oh, Jon only had to pay for it to be re-set,' she replied airily. 'The diamond is one of his family's heirlooms and what I meant is that giving it to me meant nothing to him. He didn't give it to me as a pledge of love for me but because to give a diamond to a woman is the right conventional thing to do when you've asked her to marry you and she's accepted your proposal. And Jon comes from a very conventional family.' She gave him a sidelong glance. 'You know, for a foreigner, you have a good command of American slang,' she remarked.

'Who says I'm a foreigner?' he retorted.

'I do. When you speak sometimes there's a definite accent. And then your name is strange. Are you sure you're not a Russian?'

'I'm not a Russian.' Again he was curt as if he resented her personal questions. 'If you're supposed to be getting married tomorrow morning what are you doing here? Why aren't you in your home town preparing for your wedding?'

She glanced away from him, back at the fire and frowned uneasily.

'Last night I decided I couldn't go through with the wedding,' she muttered. 'I decided I need more time to think about marriage. I felt I couldn't make promises to a man I don't love and who doesn't love me. I had to get away, be by myself for a while. So I ran away.'

'Ran away? You mean you've come here without telling him or anyone else?' he exclaimed.

'Yes. I'm like that. I do things on impulse.' She

slipped the ring off the third finger of her left hand and slid it on to the middle finger of her right hand. 'There. I'm not engaged to Jon any more. I'm free again, free to go where I like when I like, free to do what I want.' She flung her arms wide. 'Oh it's a wonderful feeling to be free again, wonderful.'

'Does this Jon know that you've broken your engagement to him?' Yvan asked. He was leaning back in his chair and regarding her with narrowed eyes. 'Have you told him?'

'Not yet. I haven't seen him since I decided I don't want to marry him.'

'Too chicken to tell him?' he suggested jeeringly.

'No. Of course not. I just didn't have time. But he'll know by now that I won't be at the church tomorrow. I called my mother and told her. I'll tell him when I go back to Renwick.'

There was another silence. He began to read again. Dandy shifted in the rocker, scowling at him. Trying to communicate with him and to find out more about him was like trying to prise open a clam. She wasn't used to dealing with such a reserved person. All the other men she knew liked to talk about themselves, but then they were all Americans like herself and were naturally gregarious, not at all secretive.

'You're very cagey,' she grumbled.

'Cagey?' He looked up in surprise.

'Secretive about yourself,' she explained. 'I'll be thinking you're in this country illegally or that you're a Russian spy, if you don't open up a little. Gramps knows all sorts of people like that.'

'Mmm. I can see from reading this book by him that he's knowledgeable about the behind-the-scenes manoeuvres of governments,' he drawled. 'But I'm not a spy nor would I want to be one. And I'm not in this country illegally. I have a valid passport and I'm here as a visitor on a weekend's vacation.'

'So?' Dandy prompted.

'So what?'

'Where do you work when you're not here?'

'In Montreal.'

'Are you a Quebeçois?' she asked, thinking she had the answer at last to his foreign accent.

'No.'

'What is your work?'

'I'm a professional engineer.'

'My stepfather, Morton Dyer is too. Electrical.'

'Dyer's Business Machines?' he queried, raising his eyebrows.

'That's right. I work for D.B.M. I'm a computer programmer. What's your discipline, as an engineer, I mean?'

His lips tightened in exasperation, he slammed his book shut and pushed his chair back. Standing up he picked up the book and began to walk across the room.

'Where are you going?' Dandy demanded.

'Away from you,' he replied nastily. 'It was to get away from prying people like you that I came here for the week-end.'

'But you'll need a light in there,' she said, springing up from the rocker and going over to the dresser. 'Wait, I'll give you a candle.'

She found a candle in a drawer, stuck it in an old brass candle-holder and finding matches lit it.

'Here you are,' she said going towards him. He had stopped in the open doorway of the back bedroom and was watching her. Shielding the flame of the candle with one hand she smiled at him, still determined to get close to him somehow and be revenged on him for kissing her against her will. 'I'll put it on the bedside table,' she added, and slipped past him into the bedroom.

Yellow candlelight danced on the warm brown walls of the room as she moved towards the bedside table. She set the candle-holder down and bending over the bed folded back the hand-made patchwork quilt.

'What are you doing?' Yvan's voice rasped harshly behind her.

'I'm just turning down the bed ready for you to get into it, as a good hostess should,' she replied smoothly. 'And making sure you have everything you need.'

'But you're not the hostess here.'

'I am when Gramps isn't here to be host,' she said lightly, but she was finding that her deliberate attempts to provoke him were causing her pulses to throb with excitement and a strange heat was flooding through her body.

The sheets turned back she swung round to face him. He was standing very close to her, his hands on his hips, his eyes glittering beneath slanting black lashes, his lips still tight with exasperation. She was so close to him she could see the black bristles of his beard, that was beginning to grow, and the smooth texture of the cream-pallored skin that was stretched taut across his cheekbones. She could also see dark lines etched below his eyes.

And she was so close to him she was sure he must be aware of the feminine scents of her hair and skin—as long as they weren't smothered by the smell of mothballs that still clung to the nightgown, she thought wryly. Dressed as she was she was hardly seductive. If only he would look down at the tantalising cleft between her breasts he might be tempted to touch her. Lifting her head she smiled at him warmly, her teeth, perfectly shaped now after those desperate years of wearing braces, glinting against the smooth redness of her lips, her long lashes dropping over her dark eyes.

'I wasn't really prying, Yvan,' she said softly, her voice deep and she said his name exactly as he had pronounced it. 'I'm interested in you, sincerely interested and . . .'

'Get out.' He spoke through his teeth but his breathing had quickened and he was looking at her mouth and he didn't move away from her.

'Are you sure there isn't anything else you need?' she whispered and swayed slightly towards him, although she hadn't intended to. Strange sensations were flickering through her body and the heat flooding through her was melting all her self-protective instincts. She was now aching for him to kiss her again. Her heart was beating loudly and it seemed to be swelling up, closing her throat. Slowly, without thinking, she put out her tongue and licked her drying lips.

'I said get out,' he rasped again.

'And if I don't, what will you do?' she challenged huskily.

'Kiss you again.' The rasping sound had gone from his voice. He bent his head closer to hers. 'And you know how much you dislike being kissed,' he taunted thickly. 'Better go now while you can.'

The whole scene was getting out of hand, not

going the way she had planned it at all, she thought wildly. It was as if he had guessed what she was trying to do and was playing with her.

'Are you going?' he asked and there was a subtle threat in the way he moved closer to her and put his hands lightly on her waist.

'I . . . I . . . can't,' she muttered.

She knew it was time for her to back off but her legs and feet wouldn't obey the orders given to them by her brain. Her head tipped back involuntarily so that her mouth with its slightly parted lips was lifted to his and her breasts were hardening and lifting too. Through the veil of her lashes she saw his eyes lose their cold clarity and blaze with blue fire. Then his lips were moving against hers, nibbling their softness and his tongue was tasting the sweetness of hers.

A long sigh shook through her, her eyes closed and she pressed against him, all thoughts of revenge fading from her mind. No man had ever kissed her in this way before and the strangest part of it was she didn't want to object or resist because she could sense in him the same aching need to make love that she was feeling.

His lips left hers and trailed hungrily down her throat. His tongue licked the smooth column of white skin. She groaned with pleasure, her body arching against his. Her hands thrust through the silkiness of his hair. He raised his head. His breath was hot on her skin.

'Do you still want me to get out?' she whispered.

'No,' he murmured. 'But I'm not going to let you stay either.'

'But I want to stay with you. And I know you want me to. I can feel that you do.' She passed her hand down over his chest over his flat stomach and downward so that he gasped sharply. 'You want me and I want you,' she whispered, winding her arms about his neck and pressing closely against him, rubbing her softness against his hardness.

He exclaimed softly in another language, twined one hand in her hair, jerking her head back. This time his lips were hard and hot, mercilessly devouring the quivering generous sweetness of hers until she became dizzy.

Through the haze of sensuousness that filmed her mind she was aware that he had lifted her and she knew a flicker of triumph. This was what she had been hoping he would do. She had hoped he would carry her to the bed lay her down and lie beside her and make love to her, showing her the way to the culmination of passion so that at last she would find out what the mystery of sexual desire was all about. She wound her arms even more tightly about him and snuggled her face against his throat, sniffing the scents of his skin, inhaling them as if they were a drug.

Then shockingly and surprisingly she was dropped on to her feet. Contact with the hard floor jolted upwards painfully from her bare heels. His arms left her. Staggering a little she opened her eyes. She was facing the open doorway of the bedrooom and was looking into the firelit, lamplit living room.

'What . . .' she began, breaking off chokingly when she was pushed hard from behind so that she rushed forward into the living room. Recovering her balance quickly she swung round to face him, words of protest springing to her lips. The words were never spoken because the door slammed in her face and while she stared at it in open-mouth bewilderment Yvan slid the bolt home on the other side. He had locked her out.

Humiliation was like a drenching cold shower sweeping over her, cooling the flames of desire. Tears pricked her eyes unexpectedly. The revenge she had planned had boomeranged. She was the one who had been repulsed.

Biting her lips to stop them from trembling she gave her shoulders a shake. She wasn't going to cry. She hadn't cried for years. She walked back to the rocking chair and sat in it again, staring into the fire, rocking herself back and forth, trying to soothe her violently disturbed emotions. Many times in her life she had experienced rejection of her impulsive offers of friendship, but never before had she offered love as she had offered it tonight to Yvan and never before had rejection seared her like this, making her feel raw and exposed.

Why had she wanted to make love with Yvan? Why want a stranger? Was it because he was handsome in a foreign way? Or because he was mysterious and she wanted to know more about him? Or was it because they were alone together, cooped up in this small cabin, cut off by a snowstorm from other people? Had propinquity, her nearness to him, set off the fireworks of desire that had been lying dormant for so long in the hidden places of her body?

Suddenly she clutched at her head and a feeling of embarrassment swept over her as she re-membered her own shamelessly wanton behaviour. God, what must he be thinking of her? He must be thinking she was no better than a sex-starved man-chaser. He must be thinking she was one of those women who made up to any man who happened to be around.

She groaned in agony. What had she done? She didn't want him to think badly of her. Quite the reverse. She wanted him to like her, but how could she convince him now that her desire to stay the night with him and make love with him had been a sincere impulse on her part, a warm and loving response to the need to be loved which she had sensed lay buried in him.

After a while she left the chair and closed the doors of the stove. She turned out the lamp on the table. Soft yellow light slanted from the open doorway of her grandfather's room where she had left the other lamp. She went into the bedroom and closed the door. Pulling back the bedclothes she nerved herself against the icy feel of the sheets and slid between them. In a few minutes she was fast asleep.

CHAPTER THREE

DANDY was awakened by the throb of the oil furnace coming on in the basement under the room where she had slept. Opening her eyes she blinked at the brilliant daylight that was streaming into the room through the double-glazed window. Bright sunlight was bouncing off white snow. The storm was over and the sky was azure and cloudless.

Flinging back the covers she slid off the bed and ran to the window. Thick snow covered everything outside. Smooth, white and untouched, it rolled in perfectly sculptured curves away to the bluish blur of trees on the horizon. It glistened yellow where the sunlight shone on it and was a soft violet in the shadow of the trees. Under its weight the down-drooping green branches of the spruce trees planted close to the cabin trembled slightly.

Grooves made by skis curved in the snow from the cabin door in the direction of the red-painted generator shed. Now she knew why the furnace had come on and why the bedroom was no longer like the inside of a refrigerator. Yvan was up and had been out to fix the small gasoline engine which drove the generator.

In the living room sunlight slanted along the log walls and glittered on the taps in the kitchen area. The smell of coffee perking filled the air. The woodstove had been cleaned out and a new fire had been set, ready for lighting. She unplugged the coffee maker, poured some liquid into a mug and sipped as she leaned against the sink unit.

Yvan had been busy. He had fixed the generator, had his breakfast, laid a fire, tidied up and had left coffee perking for her.

It's so nice to have a man about the house, she sang to herself, especially when he's practical. She opened the fridge to see if anything had been spoilt while the electricity had been off then swung the door closed sharply and stopped singing as she realised how quiet the cabin was. Yvan wasn't indoors. Then where was he?

Perhaps, irritated by her behaviour of the night before, he had left. Oh, she did hope he hadn't. She wanted to see him again. She hurried to his bedroom. The door was partly open. If he had left he would have taken his belongings with him, wouldn't he?

She entered the room and let out a sigh of relief when she saw that he had left the sweater and pants he had been wearing the night before in a chair. She looked around and stepped towards the clothes closet. She pushed open the door. Clothing hung on hangers and on the floor there was a suitcase. She lifted the case. It came up easily. It was empty.

He hadn't left. He was still about somewhere, probably still in the generator shed. On her way to the door she passed the chest of drawers. On top of it Yvan had left a few personal items; a ring of keys, a leather wallet and a thin dark blue book embossed with the Canadian coat of arms with the word PASSPORT in English and also in French.

She picked up the passport and opened it. Flicking over the first page she found a photograph of Yvan looking very cool and haughty. On the page facing the photograph was a description of the bearer of the passport.

'Yvan Rambert,' she read. Her glance slid down to the next line. Date of Birth. She calculated rapidly. Yvan was thirty-one, ten years older than herself, and he had been born in Paris, France, on the last day of November.

She put the passport back on the chest and turned towards the door, gasping with surprise when she saw Yvan standing in the doorway watching her with cold, hostile eyes. Her heart sank. He had caught her prying and she had been hoping so hard that she would be able to put herself in the right with him by explaining how she had felt last night. Now he would be thinking even more badly of her and he would really want to leave.

He was coming towards her, a threat in every stride. He was wearing an all-black ski suit which somehow made him seem even more menacing, a devil with chips of ice for eyes. But she didn't back away from him. It wasn't in her to back away from danger of any sort.

'There is an explanation, that is if you'd care to listen to it,' she said, tilting her head back and secretly wishing she wasn't wearing the ridiculous nightgown.

'So, go ahead. Explain,' he replied tautly, standing in front of her, his hands on his hips. Although he looked as if he hadn't slept much he was cleanly shaven and his hair was brushed, its blackness glinting with blue lights.

'I didn't come in here to pry,' she began.

'The why come in at all?'

'I thought you'd left, so I came in to check if your belongings were here.'

'You really expect me to believe you?' he challenged.

'I don't much care if you do or not,' she flared suddenly. 'But it's true. And I was just leaving when I saw your passport. I couldn't help looking at it. I wanted to know your last name and which country you're from.' She gave him a defiant glare. 'Well, you wouldn't tell me anything about yourself so I had to find out on my own. If you'd been less cagey last night I wouldn't have looked at your passport.' He didn't say anything so she continued rather self-righteously. 'You know I'm getting the impression you don't want me to know anything about you because you've done something wrong. Have you? Are you afraid I might recognise your name? Well, you needn't be. I don't. We don't get much news of what goes on in Canada down here. What have you done? Robbed a bank?'

'No.' He almost spat the word at her. 'I'm not a spy and I'm not a thief.'

'Then are you a member of that separatist movement in Quebec? What's it called?' Dandy snapped her fingers as she tried to recall the name. 'I know. I remember the initial letters now. The F.L.Q. Are you a member of it?'

'No. I am not. I do not care for politics or terrorist organisations.' His breath hissed as he drew it in. 'As you have seen I was born in France and I'm now a Canadian citizen. What else do you need to know?' He paused, then snarled softly, 'You're a damned nuisance, you know that? And if we have to spend today and tonight in this cabin

I don't want you to come into this room again. Is that clear?'

She nodded and he turned away as if intending to leave the room, but he didn't. He swung back to face her. He looked at her as if he hated her and something within her cried out against that bitter look. If another man had looked at her like that she would have shrugged her shoulders. But she didn't want Yvan to hate her. She wanted him to like her, possibly to love her.

'I'm sorry,' she said simply. 'And I promise I won't come in here again.' He continued to frown at her so she stepped forward and placed a hand on his arm. 'Oh, Yvan, why can't we be friends?' she whispered.

He shook off her hand and turned towards the door again, then looked back at her.

'Why the hell did you have to come here while I'm here?' he asked wearily. 'Why couldn't you have run away to some other place? I had really hoped to be alone for a couple of days.'

'There was no other place I could go and anyway Gramps said I could always come here.' A sudden rage of frustration surged through her because he was once again spurning her. 'I can't help being what I am,' she blurted. 'I can't help being friendly and outgoing, and curious about the people I meet. I want to know about you because ... because ... well, to tell the truth, I like you very much.'

'How can you possibly know that you like me ... very much? We met for the first time last night and our meeting was not at all friendly,' he said dryly but it seemed to her that his manner had softened slightly, encouraging her to say more.

'I know I like you because I have this feeling here.' She thumped a fist against the place in her chest where she believed her heart ought to be. 'And when you kissed me ... I mean the second time you kissed me, in this room, when you kissed me as if you wanted to kiss me and liked kissing me, I didn't pull away or hit you as I'd intended to. I let you go on kissing me and I would have let you do more. I was willing to go all the way with you. But you put me out as if I'd been a stray kitten or puppy that had wandered into your room.'

Surprise widened his eyes and his slanting eyebrows went up.

'Are you telling me that you deliberately set out to tempt me to kiss you so that you could hit me?' he exclaimed. 'My God, you are a very strange woman. Why would you want to do something like that?'

'I was trying to be revenged on you for the way you kissed me when we were fighting,' she muttered and even to her ears her explanation sounded ridiculous.

'Revenge for what reason?' he asked, looking puzzled. 'I do not understand you.'

'No, I don't suppose you do ... because you're not a woman,' she said bitterly. 'You see when you used such an underhand way to defeat me by kissing me to make me stop fighting you ... you humiliated me and so I wanted to humiliate you in some way ... but instead I was humiliated again for the second time when you put me out of this room.'

She broke off because her voice was shaking and turned away to look out of the window at the

dazzle of sunlight on snow. Behind her silence
stretched to twanging point and she was beginning
to think he would never say anything when he
spoke quietly, almost kindly, as he might have
spoken to a child.

'I didn't intend to humiliate you. I have told you
why I kissed you the first time. It was so I
wouldn't have to defend myself by hitting you.
And the second time, you are right, I did want to
kiss you and would have liked to have gone on
kissing you. I would have liked to have taken you
into my bed and made love to you.' He paused,
then added roughly. 'I put you out of the room for
your own protection, not to humiliate you.'

'My protection?' She whirled round to face him.
'What were you protecting me against?'

'Myself.' His lips twisted in self-mockery. 'It's
been a while since I was intimate with a woman
and by behaving the way you did you were risking
being taken against your will.'

'No, no. It wouldn't have been like that,' she
said urgently. 'It wouldn't have been against my
will. Oh, that's what I want to explain to you. I
want to tell you how I felt. Oh, please wait and
listen to me.' He had started to turn away again.
She sidled past him until she was in front of him
and they were facing each other again. 'It's never
happened to me before,' she whispered a strange
shyness coming over her now that she was
committed to making an explanation. 'I think I've
fallen in love for the first time in my life. I've fallen
in love with you.'

'In love with *me*?' He laughed jeeringly. 'Now I
know you are crazy. You've known me only a few
hours so you can't possibly be in love with me.'

Mockery faded from his face and he looked very stern. 'You must not be in love with me. I'm not a suitable person for you to be in love with.'

'But I am. I am in love with you,' she insisted. 'I know I am because no man has ever made me tingle with desire the way you have. No man has ever turned me on before.'

'Not even your fiancée?'

'Not even Jon. Oh, I've been kissed by him and by other men friends but nothing has ever happened inside me before, like it did when you kissed me. I'm not in love with Jon and never have been. That's why I've decided not to marry him. Marriage to him would be one big bore. He doesn't light me up.'

'And I do?' His upper lip lifted in a sneer.

'You did last night,' she whispered. 'You do now. I wish you'd kiss me again.'

For a moment she thought he was going to do as she had asked because his lips parted and his head tipped towards hers. Then he drew in his breath harshly and stepped back from her.

'Stop it, stop trying to seduce me,' he cautioned her. 'You're promised to Jon.' His face seemed to have gone several shades paler and bone showed through skin at the angle of his jaw as he gritted his teeth.

'I've already broken my promise to Jon by running away,' she retorted. 'And I'm not trying to seduce you. I'm trying to show you how much I like you. Please try to understand. The feeling keeps bubbling up inside me wanting to spill over. I can't contain it. And I'm not a child any more. I'm not a sex-starved teenager indulging in a fantasy. I'm a grown woman, free to do what I

want, free to fall in love and make love if I want
to. You don't have to protect me against yourself
and you don't have to take any responsibility for
my actions or behaviour. I can look after myself.
So if you feel again you would like to kiss me and
make love to me, don't hold back, because I'm
more than willing to make love with you, but only
with you.'

He stared at her, his expression puzzled, then
slowly his lips curved in a faint enigmatic smile.

'I am honoured,' he replied with a slight
mocking bow. 'But right now I prefer to go ski-
ing. The conditions are perfect for cross-country.'

'I'll come with you,' she said eagerly.

'You will of course do what you want to do
since you are free to do it,' he retorted jeeringly. 'I
can't stop you.'

Turning on his heel he strode from the room. A
few seconds later the door of the cabin slammed.
He was going to go without her. Dandy let out a
groan of frustration and beat her head with her
fists. She had made a mess of everything again.
Her openness and honesty had offended him.

Hurrying into the living room she grabbed her
dried clothes from the chairs and rushed to the
bathroom. She showered and dressed quickly, then
ate cereal in the kitchen area. She rinsed the bowl
she had used then dashed to the trap door in the
floor, flashlight in hand and went down the ladder
to the basement where she knew some old skis and
boots were stored.

The skis and the boots that fitted her were in
fairly good condition and she knew she had her
grandfather to thank for that. She carried them up
to the living room, waxed them and placed them

near the door ready for when she wanted to leave. Going to the kitchen area she made some sandwiches, took two cans of fruit juice from the fridge and packed them with the sandwiches in the small nylon backpack she had found in the basement.

From the chest in her grandfather's bedroom she took a pair of his thick woollen socks and a pair of nylon-covered thick ski-ing mitts. Back in the living room she put on the ski-boots laced them up and pulled the woollen sock on over them for extra warmth and protection. She slung the backpack on her shoulders, pulled on the mitts and collecting her poles and skis stepped outside.

When the skis were on she grasped the poles and set off in the kick-glide rhythm, which she had perfected over several years of cross-country ski-ing, and followed the tracks which Yvan had made.

The sun shone out of the ice blue sky and struck diamond sparks from the snow. There was no wind. The only sound apart from the squeak of the skis passing over the snow was the twitter of small birds as they hopped from branch to branch of the silver birches that were scattered about the gently rolling land behind the cabin.

After following Yvan's tracks for nearly an hour she had to admit that he had made the most of his start and was far ahead of her. Resting in an open glade in the forest she drank from one of the cans of juice and ate a sandwich, and thought broodingly about him.

He didn't want her company. He didn't like her. He probably thought she was vulgar and lacking in sensitivity because she had confessed she had

fallen in love with him. Oh, why couldn't she
control her tongue? Why couldn't she behave with
more sublety? be more feminine, her mother would
have said.

Should she go on and hope to find him resting
somewhere and then have the heart-tugging, sense-
titillating pleasure of returning to the cabin with
him? He couldn't have gone much further because
the trail ended on the edge of the steep-sided valley
and it was dangerous to ski down the valley slopes
on cross-country skies. She he would have to come
back this way soon. She would go and meet him.

Half an hour later she reached the end of the
trail. Yvan wasn't in sight. Leaning on her poles
she looked down the steep slope to a tangle of
trees clustering about the frozen course of the
small river that flowed through the valley. Ski-
tracks curved down the slope towards the trees.
Yvan had gone where she had been warned not to
go by her grandfather because she might fall and
break a leg or she might collide with tree stumps
or a hidden rock and knock herself out.

The danger of ski-ing the slope hadn't prevented
Yvan from going down it so why should it stop
her? Grasping her poles she began to glide down
the slope. A movement among the trees caught
her eye and she ploughed to a stop. A black figure
was gliding along beside the river. She cupped her
hands about her mouth and shouted to him. He
stopped, turned and looked up. She waved a pole
at him and shouted. 'I'm coming down. Wait for
me.'

It wasn't easy following his tracks but at last she
passed the rocky outcrops and tiny rock-clinging
bushes. There was a smooth stretch of open snow

before her sloping down to the river. Confidently she pushed forwards and gradually began to pick up speed as if she were on downhill skis. Desperately she dug her poles into the snow to try and stop and was thinking of throwing herself sideways into the snow when one of her skis hit a hidden rock and she was catapulted forward. Over she went in a slow somersault to land jarringly on her back.

She lay still, afraid to move in case she had broken a leg or an arm. She stared up at the sky. A faint rose-colour was beginning to stain the bright hard blue, warning her that the sun had begun to set. She wondered if Yvan had seen her fall. Would he come to help her? Or had he gone on after she had waved to him?

Slowly she raised her head then let it fall back. Yvan was coming. She had seen his head and shoulders showing above the curve of the snowy slope. Her heart raced and her mouth curled in a mischievious grin. Closing her eyes she let her lips fall open as if she were unconscious. This might be the time to be more subtle, a little helpless.

His ski suit rustled as he knelt beside her. She raised her lashes a little and looked sideways. He was sitting down and removing his skis so that he could move about her more easily. When the skis were off and had been thrust into the snow he turned towards her and she lowered her lashes quickly.

'Dandy?' He spoke softly and she guessed he was kneeling beside her. She liked the way he said her name. He lengthened the 'a' and shortened the 'y' so that it sounded like 'Dondi'—A chic French name something like 'Gigi', she thought. Then she

nearly gave herself away because he placed the
back of his bare hand against her cheek and his
touch was like an electric shock. Gently he stroked
her cheek with his knuckles and she held her
breath. 'Dandy,' he said again. 'Are you hurt?'

She couldn't hold her breath any longer so she
let it out in a sort of groan and moved her head
from side to side. The excited thump of her heart
seemed to fill her ears drowning out any other
sound as she waited for his next move. She knew
when he moved because his shadow no longer lay
across her eyelids, so she opened her eyes a little.
He was beginning to take the ski off her left foot.
She closed her eyes again, bracing herself for pain
when he touched her leg to find out if it was
broken.

There was no pain and he was able to
straighten her left leg so that it lay beside her
right leg. He took the ski off her right foot and
she felt his fingers probing her ankle and moving
up her leg. Again there was no pain. Neither of
her legs was broken. He felt her arms with the
same result.

After that he was quiet for so long she opened
her eyes to see what he was doing. She closed them
quickly because he was sitting close to her looking
down at her face. Seconds passed in silence. The
air grew colder. Dandy could hear the snow
creaking as it froze and she could feel the tips of
her fingers and her toes growing numb. Her
uncovered ears were also tingling. She would have
to move soon to keep her circulation going. She
didn't want to get frost-bite, so she groaned again
and let her eyelashes flutter.

'You can stop pretending.' Yvan's voice was

dry. 'I know you're not unconscious and as far as I can tell you haven't broken anything.'

She opened her eyes wide. Against the snow, now rose-coloured like the sky, he was a black shape.

'Except the back of my head and my neck,' she moaned. 'Oh I think I might have broken my neck. It hurts to turn it.'

'If you had broken your neck you wouldn't be turning your head or speaking to me,' he retorted, unsympathetically. 'But I'm surprised you didn't break something, the way you came down the slope.'

'I wanted to catch up with you. I've been trying to catch up with you all afternoon. But you went so fast.'

'Come on, sit up,' he ordered. 'I'll help you to put your skis on.'

'I don't think I can move,' she whispered. 'Please will you help me to sit up?'

Taking hold of her shoulders he jerked her up into a sitting position.

'You don't have to be so rough,' she complained. 'My head and neck really do hurt.' She rubbed the back of her neck with one hand. 'I think I must have landed on it when I somersaulted.'

'Here?' His voice had changed. He spoke softly and she felt his hand lifting her thick hair away from the back of her neck. His fingertips touched then stroked her nape. Downwards they stroked and slid under the rolled collar of her sweater to caress the top of her spine. Delicious tingles danced along her nerves and she lifted her head quickly to look at him. Her cheek brushed against his jaw, another sense-arousing contact that made her gasp. He withdrew sharply from the contact, the bristles of his beard scraping the smoothness of her skin and he turned his head to look at her. His lips less than an inch from hers he said,

'Did I touch the right place?'

'Yes, oh yes,' she sighed. 'Please do it again. It was delicious.'

He laughed gruffly and touched the back of her neck again, his fingers moving sensuously against her skin. Her eyelids dropped as she looked at his lips so close to her own and saw them part, saw the tip of his tongue red and moist before his mouth covered hers hungrily.

His kiss bruised her lips and drained from her mouth all the sweetness it had to offer him and although Dandy realised he was taking and not giving anything in return she didn't care. Response to his demand bubbled up within her and overflowed. No longer did she feel cold, for his touch had lit a flame in her which blazed up, consuming caution and commonsense. She felt alive in a way she had never felt before and the desire to show him that he was more than welcome to take what she had to offer throbbed through her so strongly that she swayed under its onslaught. He swayed with her and they collapsed together on the snow, the crisp surface giving way under their combined weights so that they were crouched on a bed of feathery softness.

As light as snowflakes but as hot as cinders his lips explored her face then returned to her mouth. A sweet heat flooded through her, melting her bones, softening her all over, but when his hand moved under her sweater, the fingers curving to the roundness of a breast, her body grew taut and thrust against his in demand so that they rolled together over and over in the snow, each trying to dominate the other, stopping at last as if by mutual consent to lie facing each other like two halves of a whole.

'We can't do it here,' he whispered against her cheek.

'Yes, we can, we can. I want to.' She twisted against him, her legs twining with his.

'No, we'll freeze to death,' he said, laughing a little. 'Let's go back to the cabin, where it's warm and comfortable.'

He sat up, pulling her with him and in the glow of the sunset they gazed at each other, eyes glazed with longing, swaying towards each other again as if they could not bear to be separated, and their lips met in another hot, sense-inflaming kiss.

Yvan moved away first, pulling his mouth from hers. Her emotions rose up and boiled over. She grasped hold of his jacket to stop him from standing up.

'I love you,' she cried.

'No, you don't.' He rejected her confession harshly, pulling her hands away from his jacket. 'This . . . what we've been doing here in the snow has nothing to do with love.'

'It does for me,' she argued.

'But not for me,' he retorted cruelly dropping her hands and standing up. He looked down at her. 'Love, true love, real love doesn't flare up suddenly for no reason at all. And it's much more than wanting to have sex with someone which is what you and I are wanting right now.'

'How do you know?' she demanded. 'Have you ever loved a woman, truly and really?'

'Yes, I have,' he said in a low voice and turning away tramped over to the skis which were standing in a row where he had thrust them into the snow.

Dandy stood up. She felt giddy and there seemed to be a hammer banging regularly and painfully at the back of her head. Yvan came back to her with her skis and laid them on the snow before her. She stepped on to them and he snapped the bindings over the toes of her boots. Then he brought her poles, handing them to her in silence, not looking at her, his face impassive, and she wondered how he could be so cold and controlled after the way they had kissed and fondled each other.

She pulled on her mitts, flexing her fingers inside them. The sky was pale grey now, except where darkness was beginning to spread over it like the wing of a great blue-black bird, and trees were a bluish blur. Close at hand the snow gleamed with a silvery light.

Watching Yvan put on his skies her thoughts were suddenly muddled by a dark evil current. He had said he loved another woman. She ground her teeth and bit back abusive words. Jealousy was a new experience for her. Never had she felt like this before, as if she could scratch out the eyes of the woman he loved.

'Why isn't she with you?' she demanded as he glided towards her over the snow.

'Who?'

'The woman you love. If you love her truly and really why haven't you brought her to stay with you at the cabin?' she said acidly.

He didn't answer but bent swiftly to check one of the bindings on his skis, thus deliberately avoiding her curious probing stare. When he straightened up his face was hard and his eyes were blank as if a steel door had shut down at the back of them.

'Do you think you can climb back up the slope?' he asked, freezingly polite.

'I'll try.' The jealous feeling was still there, a black cloud hovering over her, darkening everything and spoiling their tenuous friendship already.

'I'll go first,' he said. 'Keep as close to me as you can and follow exactly in my tracks, then you won't collide with any hidden rocks. I wouldn't like you to fall again.'

He began to climb the slope and she followed him.

'But Yvan, if you love her, truly and really, how can you . . .' she began, unable to keep quiet, but breaking off when he spun round to face her, his skis churning up snow. His face was livid, almost as white as the snow and the blaze in his eyes frightened her.

'Shut up,' he snarled. 'Stop asking so many damn-fool questions. Save your breath for the trip back to the cabin. You're going to need it. Now, come on. It's cold and if we stand around much longer we'll both get frost-bite.'

He went up the slope as if demons were chasing him and suppressing an inclination to shout curses after him Dandy followed, every move she made jolting her bruised and aching joints and muscles. It was harder going up the slope than coming down it had been and often she slid back as many steps as she had taken forward. Only a fierce determination to show the man in front that she could do what he could do kept her going. She refused to be beaten.

At the top of the slope he waited for her and together they glided along the trail. The moon came up over the tops of the trees and peered at them, lighting the way. Twice Dandy fell and twice Yvan helped her up and brushed snow from her clothing and they set off again together. But she couldn't keep up with him and she longed to ask him to stop and wait for her while she rested. But she didn't. Gritting her teeth she stayed silent, a stubborn, native pride refusing to let her give in to weakness.

By the time she could see the cabin and the frozen lake beyond it Yvan was a good quarter of a mile in front of her and moving across the open land towards the cabin. When she at last reached the pathway he was in the house and light was slanting out through the windows. There was the smell of woodsmoke. Not more than twenty-four hours had passed since she had arrived at the cabin but Dandy felt as if she had aged about ten years.

Outside the door of the cabin she removed her skis and when she straightened up her head seemed to spin. She staggered to the door and pushed it open. Heat from the room within wafted out to her, welcoming her. Concentrating hard she stepped forward, but a sort of fog filled her brain, blurring everything.

'Yvan,' she called, and crashed to the floor.

CHAPTER FOUR

SHE didn't black out completely, but it was a while before the ceiling stopped revolving and she was able to focus her eyes on Yvan's face as he knelt beside her.

'What happened?' he asked.

'Everything went foggy and spun around me. Oh, I know you don't believe anything I say but I really did bang the back of my head when I fell. I could have concussion.'

'Then you must go to bed and rest,' he said firmly. 'But first you must get out of those clothes and then you must have a hot bath. Here, I'll help you.'

He helped her to her feet and guided her into the front bedroom, pushing her down to sit on the side of the bed. Kneeling before her he removed her ski-boots and her long knee socks. He plumped up two pillows against the headboard and told her to lean against them. She obeyed him meekly, surprised at her own submissiveness. He lifted her legs on to the bed and began to unbuckle the belt which held her pants up.

'What are you doing?' she gasped, rearing up so suddenly that her head reeled.

'Helping you to get out of these wet clothes,' he replied practically, jerking the end of the belt out of the buckle. He unzipped her pants and dizzy, unable to protest, Dandy slumped back against the pillows and let him ease the pants down over her hips. He drew them off and dropped them on to the floor. She struggled to sit up again.

'I can undress myself, thank you,' she said with dignity.

'Now for your jacket,' he said crisply as if she hadn't spoken and peeled the jacket from her carefully. It was also dropped to the floor. 'And now for your sweater,' he added. 'Lift your arms up.'

Knowing that she had nothing on under the sweater because she never wore a bra Dandy leaned back against the pillows again.

'I'm not completely helpless,' she retorted. 'I'll take it off myself. Please go away.'

'No.'

'But I can really manage by myself now. I don't feel dizzy any more.'

'Then you have recovered very quickly,' he remarked with a glint of mockery. He leaned towards her and taking hold of the ribbed waistband of the sweater began to lift it. 'Come on, lift your arms,' he whispered. 'If we were making love right now you wouldn't care if I did undress you, would you?'

'But we're not making love,' she replied in a choked voice. She was out of her depth now, not knowing whether the swimming of her senses was caused by the bang on her head or by his nearness, the scents of his skin and hair, the warmth of his breath on her cheek, the touch of his fingertips on her bare waist. 'Oh, please go away. I don't feel like letting you see me with nothing on.'

He laughed, that soft yet gruff sound which came from the depths of his throat and possessed such a suggestive quality.

'It won't be the first time I've seen a woman without anything on,' he murmured. 'I'm not an inexperienced youth getting thrills from peeping at nude women.'

'Oh, I don't suppose I would be the first with you,' she flared, glaring at him. 'I guess you've seen lots and lots of women with nothing on and had lots and lots of lovers too.'

'Not lots and lots,' he said, with a touch of amusement. 'You see I'm no more a libertine hopping from one woman's bed to another than you are a woman of easy virtue, in spite of your efforts to convince me that you are.'

'I . . . I . . . oh, I haven't been trying to convince you that I'm easy,' she spluttered, all her aches and pains forgotten temporarily in a surge of irritation because he had misunderstood her.

'No?' His eyebrow twitched derisively. 'Yet this morning you went to a lot of trouble to make sure I was aware you're available if I feel I want to have sex with you while we're staying here together. And this afternoon, on the hillside after you had fallen you showed me you're available.'

'But only because . . . because . . . I . . . oh, I hate you. I hate you. Go away, go away,' she cried out furiously, stung by his mockery of her.

'Yet not much more than an hour ago you told me you love me,' he chided her and sighed exaggeratedly. 'I'm glad I didn't believe you. *Varium et mutabile semper femina.*'

'What does that mean? What are you saying about me?' she demanded.

On his way to the bedroom door with her wet clothes hanging over one arm he turned to glance at her.

'Didn't you study Latin at school?' he queried, looking superior. 'I was quoting from Virgil's *Aeneid*. He said woman is always fickle and changing. How right he was.'

'Pig,' she yelled at him. 'Chauvinistic French pig.' And pulling one of the pillows from behind her she hurled it across the room too late. It hit the closed door and fell to the floor. He had gone.

Damn! Damn! Damn! Dandy pounded the bed with her fists. Everything was going wrong, as was usual with her. She had wanted so much for this evening to be different. She had hoped after the way he had kissed her on the hillside, after the way passion had flamed between them in the snow, that he would have taken her offer of love and friendship seriously and that they would have slept together tonight.

But now she had probably offended him even more by implying that he was immoral in his dealings with women. That hadn't been what she had meant, though, when she had said she guessed he had had lots and lots of lovers. Nor had she intended to call him a pig. Some time later she would tell him what she had meant. She would apologise and explain, begin all over again with him.

There was a sharp knock on the door. It opened a little.

'I've run water into the bath for you,' Yvan said through the opening. 'Go and get in it while it is hot. I'm cookng some dinner for us. When you've bathed come and eat.'

The door closed again. Painfully Dandy slid off the bed and went over to the blanket chest. She took out one of her grandfather's shirts, thinking it would be easier to put on than the nightgown and would act as a sort of dressing robe, then leaving the bedroom she went along to the bathroom.

Some time later, her joints and muscles soothed by the hot water, although her head still ached and her shoulders and neck were sore, dressed in her panties and her grandfather's shirt, which came down past her knees, she sat down at the table in the living room. Yvan had pulled the table close to the stove, the doors of which were open, showing bright flames leaping up from birch logs. One of the oil lamps standing in the centre of the table sent out soft yellow beams over table mats and silverware.

Yvan set down a plate in front of her. She looked down at a delicate golden brown envelope on the plate. From it oozed tiny mushrooms.

'I hope you like omelette,' Yvan said sitting down opposite her and opening a bottle of white wine.

'It looks very good,' she murmured, over-awed by his competence in the kitchen. She helped herself to bread and butter while he poured wine into one of the glasses. He looked across at her.

'I would like to offer you some wine but I think it best if you don't drink any tonight. It would not be good for you to drink it after being slightly concussed,' he said seriously.

'Water will do. I'm not accustomed to drinking wine at all.' She scooped up some of the omelette in her fork and ate it 'This is great,' she exclaimed. 'Who taught you to cook? Your mother?'

'No. My mother died when I was eight. I learned to cook by doing it. When I first went to live in Canada I lived by myself. And when you live alone you learn to cook quickly,' he said.

'Or you go to the fast-food restaurant down the street. Or to a take-out food place,' Dandy retorted dryly, thinking of her own bad habits when it came to getting food. 'I've lived by myself for nearly two years, ever since my stepfather threw me out, but I can't cook like you can.'

'He threw you out?' he queried in a puzzled way. 'Threw you out of where?'

'Oh, he didn't throw me out literally. He just told me to leave his house. He said he'd put up with me long enough. You see I've always been a bit rebellious against the establishment and Morton C. Dyer, my stepfather, is *very*, *very* establishment, if you know what I mean.'

'I think I do,' he murmured thoughtfully. 'He's very conventional and always does everything in the traditional way and expects members of his family to do the same.'

'That's right. That's it exactly. So ever since he asked me to get out I've had an apartment, in an old house, in Renwick. It's great being on my own and not having to please anyone else all the time.'

He made no comment nor did he look at her. She studied him from under her lashes wondering how to get through to the real person behind his cool indifferent manner.

'Yvan . . .' she ventured.

'Mmm?' He went on eating, not looking at her.

'I want to apologise : . . again. I didn't mean what you thought I meant when I said I guessed you'd had lots and lots of lovers.'

He glanced up at her his eyebrows rising in puzzlement.

'So what did I think you meant?' he asked.

'You thought I was implying that you sleep around all the time with different women, didn't you?'

'Perhaps.' He picked up the wine bottle and refilled his glass. 'If that isn't what you meant what did you mean?'

'I guess I meant that lots of women have liked and admired you ... before me,' she muttered, frowning as she wondered if she was making a mess of everything again. 'Haven't they?'

'Possibly.' He drank some wine then standing up collected up their empty plates. 'Would you like some dessert?' he asked politely. 'There is fresh fruit and cheese.'

'Oh, I do believe you haven't heard a word I've said,' she snapped crossly.

'I've heard everything you've said,' he replied smoothly.

'Then why don't you say something?'

'What would you like me to say? Actually, what you've said doesn't seem to be worthy of any comment from me.'

'I've apologised to you. The least you could do is accept my apology,' she replied haughtily.

'So. I accept your apology,' he said, inclining his head in a mock bow.

'But ... but I'm not sorry I called you a chauvinistic pig,' she hissed, goaded beyond control by his derisive attitude, 'because you are, you are.' She sprang to her feet and then wished she hadn't because her head throbbed agonisingly. 'Oh, what's the use of me trying to explain how I feel to you. You don't like me and you don't want to listen to me. I might as well not be here so I'm going to bed.'

'Good,' he said and she swung round to face him, glaring furiously. 'I mean, of course, it is a good idea for you to go to bed. You need rest after hurting your head,' he added, his lips twitching with amusement.

Words failed Dandy for once. Spinning on her heel she walked towards the front bedroom trying to be dignified. She slammed the bedroom door shut, picked up the pillow she had thrown at Yvan, and climbed into bed, shifting about and trying to get comfortable. Through the wall behind her she heard water running and she guessed Yvan was taking a bath or a shower. She closed her eyes, determined to sleep.

A few minutes later she opened her eyes and looked round the lamplit room. How was she going to get through the night, tormented as she was by her aching head and shoulders and by the memory of what had happened between her and Yvan on the hillside in the snow? If only she had some pills she could take to knock her out.

Tears filled her eyes and slid down her cheeks so she closed her eyes again, refusing to weep. She had never thought that falling in love could be like this, both pain and pleasure. She have never thought she would ever fall in love with a man who didn't like her. She saw herself again through Yvan's eyes and groaned. He must think she was a forward hussy, making up to him for only one reason—to have sex with him.

The latch on the bedroom door clicked and she stiffened all over, but kept her eyes closed. She heard the door shut and opened her eyes. Yvan had come into the room. He was wearing a three-quarter length blue dressing-gown. It seemed to be all he was wearing, because his chest was bare and so were his feet and the part of his legs she could see. He came to the bedside and looked down at her. His black hair was wet and sleek and he smelt of soap. More blue than grey, reflecting the colour of his robe, his eyes shimmered between black lashes. Vibrant and handsome, he was overwhelmingly masculine and attractive to her. She longed to reach out, grasp him and pull him down on top of her.

'You've been crying,' he remarked, sitting down on the side of the bed.

'I never cry,' she retorted proudly.

'Then why are your eyelashes wet?' he asked and brushed a fingertip lightly across the tips of her lashes.

'My neck and shoulders still hurt and my head aches. I don't seem to be able to relax,' she muttered. 'You wouldn't have any painkillers would you? Aspirin or Tylenol or something like that?'

'No, I haven't. I don't take drugs.'

'Nor do I usually, but I don't know how I'm going to sleep with this ache.'

'Turn over,' he ordered. 'On to your stomach.'

'Why?'

'So that I can massage your neck and shoulders.'

She looked into his eyes. Nothing there except the shimmer of blue-grey irises. No mockery. No warmth or desire either. He was making a genuine offer to help her.

She turned obediently on to her stomach and he pulled the bedclothes down to her waist.

'The shirt will have to come off,' he said. 'It's a very ugly shirt. Why are you wearing it?'

'I couldn't get my nightgown on,' she muttered keeping her face turned away from him as he slid the shirt off her shoulders and down her arms. It wasn't much more than an hour ago that she had refused to let him take her sweater off. But this was different, she argued with herself, because they weren't facing each other. When the shirt was off he told her to put her arms down close to her sides and after a while she felt his fingers against her skin. Gently his thumbs rotated at the base of her neck.

'Is that the place that hurts?' he asked.

'One of the places. But higher up too behind my ears and lower down at the top of my shoulderblades.'

First he massaged her scalp as if he were shampooing her hair until her whole head was tingling and a pleasant drowsiness weighted her eyelids and she was just floating off into sleep when he stopped. Immediately she was wide awake. She could hear him moving.

'What are you doing?' she asked. 'Please don't go yet.'

'I'm not going. Massaging is warm work so I'm taking off my robe. No, don't move. I'm going to massage your shoulders now.'

His fingertips soon found the protesting nerves in her muscles and she groaned with the pain. He began to knead her shoulders with his hands, just as if she were a lump of dough, she thought with bitter humour, as she gasped and moaned. There was nothing romantic about what he was doing to her.

'Oh, please stop,' she cried at last.

'Not yet,' he panted.

'But you're hurting me,' she complained.

'I know, but when I've finished you won't ache so much. Try to relax. Think about something else and the pain will go away.'

She closed her eyes. Slowly the pressure of his fingers grew less. She felt him shifting about and knew when he lay down beside her. Heat flowed from the skin he had massaged to her muscles, easing them. He stroked her neck again soothingly then the palm of his hand slid caressingly over her shoulders, down her back to her waist, over and over again, rhythmically and sensuously. Over her hip round to the small of her back and up again he smoothed her skin and she started to float again, out into a world of light where there was no more pain, only warmth and ease, softness . . . she slept.

Much later she opened her eyes and lay listening, sure that she had heard a voice speaking. Behind her, close behind her, someone muttered. All her senses alert she listened and felt. Someone was in bed with her, under the covers. She turned on to her back. The room was filled with grey light slanting through the window.

She glanced sideways and saw Yvan's profile, the fine edge of his nose, the droop of hair over his forehead. She reached out and her fingers touched warm skin stretched over a rib cage. Her fingers slid downwards, liking the silky feel of his skin, right down over his waist to the hard thrust of his hip bone. He was completely naked! And so was she.

He muttered something in French and she snatched her hand away from him. He turned on to his side and flung an arm across her. His hand rested lightly on her bare arm and his forearm crushed her breasts. Slowly his hand stroked her arm. His head dipped close to hers and against her throat his lips burned. Turning towards him she touched his cheek.

'Niki,' he whispered. 'Ah, Niki, *je t'aime, je t'aime beaucoup.*'

She went stiff all over. She didn't need to be a linguist to understand what he had said. *Ah, Niki, I love you, I love you very much,* he had said. He was dreaming; dreaming he was with another woman. He was making love to *her* body, caressing *her* shoulders, kissing *her* throat, but he was calling her by another woman's name. In a sort of fascinated horror she cried out in protest.

'Oh, wake up, wake up. I'm Dandy, not Niki. Oh, please wake up, Yvan.'

His hand left her shoulder and he raised his head. In the grey light of dawn he looked down at her, frowning.

'What am I doing here in bed with you?' he asked.

'You were massaging my shoulders last night and I fell asleep. You must have fallen asleep too,' she replied cautiously.

'I thought. . . .' he began and broke off to frown again. 'I must have been dreaming,' he muttered. The frown faded and his lips tilted in a slight smile. 'I remember now stroking your back,' he added. 'It was like stroking silk and doing it must have had the same soporific effect on me as it had on you. I dreamed we were making love,' he went on softly and suggestively. 'I wish we were making love.'

'So do I,' she whispered. She was no longer stiff. Nearness to him seemed to be softening her. She shifted closer to him until their hips were touching and raised her hand to the nape of his neck. His hair coiled around her fingers. 'Now we can do what we couldn't do in the snow,' she murmured.

He bent his head towards her, his face blurring as it came closer to hers. His lips were hard and hot, but they touched hers gently and his tongue licked along the smooth curves like a flame before plunging into the moistness of her mouth, possessing it passionately while his fingers moved with slow seduction over the smooth swell of her breast.

Tingling with desire she pressed her length against his hard body and touched him everywhere she could. She played with his hair, dug her nails into the smooth tautness of his skin-sheathed muscles, stroking him and pinching him until he gasped with pleasure and pushing her on to her back dominated her again with a bruising kiss.

Trapped between his hard thighs, her lips blistered by his kiss, Dandy experienced a sharp pain that was followed by a feeling of heady triumph when he became a part of her and flowed into her. He was hers at last, and then he was lying against her in breathless, heart-thudding silence, his body slack. After a while he whispered, 'I'm sorry. I couldn't hold back any longer.'

'I know,' she said shyly. 'But it was to be expected,' she added with a new wisdom and understanding that surprised her. 'You said last night that it's been some time since you've been intimate with a woman. Now perhaps you'll be able to sleep without having bad dreams.'

The words were hardly out of her mouth than she regretted them, when she saw his face grow hard. She sensed he was close to withdrawing from her in distaste and caught her lower lip between her teeth. Oh, damn, she had offended him again. She had intruded upon the privacy of his dreams about another woman and he hated her for it. Why couldn't she hold her tongue? Why did she have to spoil everything by saying the first thing that came into her head?

But, miraculously it seemed, his face softened and his lips smiled again. His eyes began to dance with a wicked kind of humour.

'Who said anything about sleeping?' he asked. 'We've slept all night. We don't need any more sleep and there's so much more for you to learn about making love, *ma belle*.'

'*Ma belle*,' she repeated dreamily. 'That means "my beautiful". Am I beautiful?' she demanded urgently. 'Do you think I'm beautiful?'

'I wouldn't call you beautiful if I did not think you are,' he replied. 'Your skin is as white as snow, pure and soft. Your hair is like black silk and your eyes are dark and deep, I could drown in them.' Bending over her he kissed her eyelids. When he raised his head his glance slanted to her mouth. 'And your lips. Ah, Dandy how can I describe your lips? They are as red and ripe as cherries and I want to bite them, suck sweetness from them.'

He began to do that and, excited and delighted already by his love-making, Dandy felt the flames of desire flare up and burn through her again. But this time he took time to arouse her, his fingers moving skilfully over her, turning hidden nerves to an exquisite throbbing pitch until she could bear the sensations no longer and felt she would go mad if there was no release from such delicate torture.

He seemed to penetrate to the very core of her and she cried out in ecstasy as all the sensations gathered together in a wonderful climax, an explosion of joy they shared together with fulfilment a sweet easing of tension, a slow spiralling down of their excitement into lazy contentment. And as the sun came up she fell asleep again, cradled in his arms.

It was the repetitive sound of a tractor going backwards and forwards, its diesel engine whining as it changed gear that wakened her several hours later. She was alone in the bed and she sat up slowly to look about her at the familiar furniture of her grandfather's room. The slant of sunlight from the far side of the window indicated that the morning was almost over.

Leaving the bed she went over to the window to look out at the snow-covered sunlit land and flung her arms wide in a gesture expressive of the sheer joy of being alive. She was in love, in love with a wonderful guy. Laughing at herself she danced across the room to pick up her grandfather's shirt from the floor. As she pulled it on she sang the song from the musical *South Pacific*, then floated about the room her arms waving up and down in time to the beat:

'*I'm in love, I'm in love, I'm in love, I'm in love with a wonderful guy,*' she sang emphatically as she pirouetted towards the doorway and collided with Yvan as he came into the room.

'So at last you wake up,' he remarked dryly. In

dark blue corduroy jeans, a dark blue turtle-necked sweater and a thin V-necked sweater of fine grey wool he looked cool and controlled. 'About time too. It is after twelve. The road to the village has been ploughed out and the guy with the plough is here now and is clearing the snow from around my car.'

'Oh, good.' She was suddenly short of words. He seemed so distant, as if they had never been close and had never made love. 'Did he say anything about my car?'

'He said he's cleared snow away from it and he asked if you are here. It seems your mother phoned his wife at the General Store and asked if you had been seen in the village. She asked if he would come out to the cabin to see if you were here.' His eyes glinted coldly as their glance swept over her. 'I wish you would get dressed and go out to show yourself to this Bill Perkins, to prove to him that you're all in one piece then he might not be so suspicious of me.'

'Yes, I will.' She shook her hair back behind her shoulders, felt a dull throb and touched the back of her head. Yvan's expression softened slightly.

'Your head still hurts?' he asked.

'Not as much.'

'And your neck and shoulders?'

'I'll survive,' she replied.

She wanted to ask him about what had happened between them early that morning. She wanted him to assure her that they had really made love and that the culmination had been as good for him as it had been for her, thanks to his expert arousal of her innate sensuality, but he was as remote from her as a mountain top and before she could think of a way to ask him he had turned away and gone back into the living room.

When she went to collect her jeans and sweater from where he had hung them to dry overnight he wasn't in the living room and the door to his bedroom was closed. She showered quickly in the bathroom, dressed and returning to the bedroom found her boots and pulled them on.

So her mother had guessed she had come to the cabin and had lost no time in phoning Jessie Perkins who owned the General Store. And Jessie had sent Bill to plough the road and find out if she was here. Dandy smiled wryly as she zipped up her boots. She couldn't do anything without everyone she knew hearing about it. Now Bill and Jessie would know she had stayed two nights in this cabin with a stranger and since it was Sunday and long-distance calls were at a cheap rate as soon as Bill told his wife what he had found at the cabin Jessie would be on the phone to Anne, to tell her that her daughter was staying at the cabin with a man who spoke English with a foreign accent.

Putting on her jacket she left the cabin and walked down the path to the tractor. The air was milder than the previous day and the sky was beginning to cloud over. A thaw had set in and the sound of dripping water was everywhere.

When he saw her Bill Perkins stopped the tractor, turned off the engine and jumped down from the cab and came towards her. A short-legged stockily built man he was wearing heavy working overalls, a check shirt and a quilted parka. A red woollen cap covered his grizzled hair and he was wearing heavy leather working gloves. His broad weather-beaten face creased into a friendly smile.

'Good to see ye, Dandy. How are yer doin'?'

'Nice to see you Bill. Is my car okay?'

'Sure is. There's still a heap of snow on the roof but you'll be able to drive it away easy enough. When did you get here?' His blue eyes were curious.

'Saturday evening, in the storm. That's why I had to abandon the car. I couldn't drive any further.'

'Jessie says Anne sounded anxious when she called last night so I came out as soon as I could this morning. I was going to leave ploughing this road until later. 'Course I knew yer grandfather's friend was here. He came Friday, bought some stores from Jessie and told us he'd be staying here for a couple of days. I guess you must have known he was here and that's why you came up,' he suggested and she nodded vaguely in agreement, not wanting to lie to him but trapped into lying by the circumstances.

'Have you heard from Gramps?' she asked casually.

'Sure have. Got a card last week. He said he'll be here end of April.'

'Do you think it'll snow again today?'

'Maybe.' He glanced up at the sky. 'When it goes colder this afternoon. Well, I'll just finish clearing the snow away from Mr Rambert's car, then I'll be on my way. Now that the road is clear you might come to the store and call your mother. She'd appreciate it if you do. See you Dandy.'

She went back into the cabin. In the kitchen area the coffee pot was half full of coffee but it needed re-heating so she plugged it in. She filled a dish with cereal, took milk from the fridge and sat down at the table to eat.

The door of the back bedroom opened and Yvan came out. He was carrying the leather suitcase she had seen in his room. He walked over to the front door of the cabin and set the case down there and turned to come back. Seeing her at the table he stopped short. Across the space separating them they stared at each other. For Dandy, troubled by his coolness after they had been so close at sunrise, the tension was unbearable. She jumped to her feet and went over to him.

'What are you doing?' she asked.

'Getting ready to leave,' he replied and swung away towards his bedroom. She followed him and leaned on the doorjamb. He gathered up his passport and other papers from the top of the chest of drawers and put them in a black briefcase.

'It . . . it didn't mean anything to you then,' she whispered. Inside she was hurting as all the joy she had felt on awakening drained out of her, leaving a raw ache somewhere between her heart and stomach.

'What didn't?' He didn't turn to look at her but snapped the locks closed on the briefcase.

'What happened . . . in bed . . . earlier this morning.' Her throat was so dry she could hardly speak.

He turned to face her. His face could have been chiselled from marble it was so pale and hard. Dandy shivered.

'It meant something,' he said coolly. 'Like most healthy men I have appetites. They were satisfied this morning.'

'But not enough,' she exclaimed, facing up to the bitterness of reality. 'I didn't satisfy you enough to make you want to stay longer here with me.' Her voice shook much to her disgust. Oh, God, she was making a mess of it again, laying herself open to more hurt. Why couldn't she behave with more pride? 'Oh, forget it,' she muttered and would have left the room but he moved swiftly to stop her, taking hold of her shoulders and swinging her around to face him again.

'Listen,' he whispered, his eyes boring into hers, his fingers gripping hard through the thickness of her jacket and sweater. 'My leaving now has nothing to do with you . . . or with what happened this morning. I had planned to leave later today and go back to Montreal. But I'm going now because the road is clear. I want to go now before it snows again and I get stuck here. I have to be in Montreal tomorrow for a meeting. I am not leaving because of what happened between you and me. Understand?' His lips curved into their slight tantalising smile. 'As a matter of fact I enjoyed what we did,' he added softly. 'You are a very warm and generous lover.'

'Then I'll come with you, to Montreal,' she offered eagerly, smiling again, pleased by the compliment. 'I'll follow you in my car. . . .'

'No.' His voice cut across hers sharply. 'You can't come with me.'

'Yes, I can. I'm free to do what I want. I have two whole weeks off from work . . . they were for the honeymoon but now. . . .'

'You can't come with me,' he insisted. 'You must go back to your home town. Don't you see, you must go back to see Jon, to tell him you don't want to marry him and to give him back his ring. You have to go back and explain. It is only fair to him and to yourself.' He drew a deep breath. 'And to me,' he added.

'But I could write to him, send the ring back by mail.'

'No, Dandy.' He was very autocratic now and frowning at her as if he disliked her. 'I don't want you to come with me. I don't want you in Montreal. Right now you'd be a complication I can do without.'

It was like a slap in the face and it brought her to her senses, revived her pride. She had told him she was able to look after herself so she wasn't going to cry and cling to him now. She forced her lips to smile and shrugged her shoulders. His hands slid away from her shoulders.

'Okay, I understand,' she said lightly. She had forgotten about the other woman, Niki, about whom he dreamed and whom he loved. Of course he wouldn't want another woman following him to Montreal and having to explain about her to Niki. Was Niki short for Nicole? 'It's been nice knowing you, Yvan,' she continued casually watching him pull on an elegant sheepskin jacket. 'Any message for Gramps?'

'I'll write him, one day,' he murmured.

She turned away quickly to leave the room and to hide from him the sudden trembling of her lips, the quick flurry of tears to her eyes.

'Dandy,' he said softly and she turned back to him, hopefully. 'It's been nice knowing you too,' he said stepping towards her. 'And always remember, that is if you have time to remember me—that I prefer to kiss you than to hurt you.'

His arms went around her, his mouth swooped to hers. Her lips parted on a sigh of pleasure and she put her arms about him. As the kiss became deeper and more passionate they rocked together from side to side and Dandy was just beginning to feel her mind slipping from her control when the front door of the cabin was flung open and Bill Perkins called out,

'Well, I'm off now, Mr Rambert, if yer want to follow me?'

Yvan dragged his lips from hers and for a moment held her tightly, his cheek pressed against her head. Then with a huskily whispered, 'I must go,' he pushed her away from him, grabbed up his briefcase and strode from the bedroom.

Shaken from head to foot by the emotional shock of their parting Dandy leaned in the doorway of the back bedroom, a hand pressed against her lips in case she cried out, and watched Yvan leave the cabin and close the door behind him. In a few moments she heard the roar of his car's engine as it started. Pushing away from the doorjamb she hurried across to the front window and watched the big yellow tractor move down the path, followed by the sleek blue car with skis tied to its roofrack. She stayed there watching until both vehicles had gone from her view. She stayed until she could hear them no more and the only sound was the incesssant dripping of melted snow.

Yvan had gone. He had shut the door and her arms were empty. He had gone and she was free to go, or stay, whatever she wished, but it was a haunted freedom because never would she forget the touch of his lips, the seduction of his fingertips,

the murmur of his voice, the slow magic of his
smile. He had gone so she would go too because
she couldn't bear to stay in this place where they
had been together and where she had learned at
last what it was like to be passionately in love.

CHAPTER FIVE

WHITE church steeples glinting against the pinkish-brown blur of leafless elm trees; red barns set on a white slant of snow-covered land; green-shuttered, white-gabled clapboard houses, those were some of the images of Vermont that Dandy left behind her as she drove southwards to Renwick.

At St Johnsbury she stopped at the same service station and was remembered by the pump attendant who asked her if she'd had good ski-ing. From the same telephone booth she called her mother collect.

'I'm coming home,' she said when Anne answered the phone. 'Should be there about nine o'clock. I'll bring your car to the house.'

'I'll be pleased to see you,' said Anne. 'Jessie Perkins called about an hour ago to say Bill had found you at Gramp's cabin.'

'I thought she would,' remarked Dandy dryly. 'See you later.'

Driving was much easier than it had been on Friday. Visibility was good and the highway was clear between high banks of snow. She kept the radio turned up loudly and drove as fast as she dared. But she didn't sing along with her favourite rock groups. She didn't sing because she was aware of a great change in herself. No longer did she feel unsure of what she was. She knew at last. She knew she was a woman with a strongly passionate nature who needed to be matched to a

92

man who could not only arouse her desire but could also satisfy it. Instinctively she had recognised that man as being Yvan as soon as he had dominated her in the karate fight.

Self-reliant, independent and strong-willed he was more than her match. He was a challenge to her own freedom-loving, outgoing personality. She needed him and she could only hope that one day he might realise he needed her.

Darkness swept across the sky. Lights twinkled from scattered farms and towns, but she didn't slow down and the clock on the dashboard was just showing nine when she turned the car off the winding river road and drove up the driveway to the Dyer house and parked in the parking space next to a red Corvette that she recognised as Jon's. She grimaced. He must be in the house, no doubt summoned by Anne and Morton when they had heard she was on her way home.

She went in by the kitchen door and sat down to remove her boots, remembering Marcie's cautionary remarks of Friday morning. *God*, Friday was another lifetime in another world. A different Dandy had returned from Vermont, an adult woman who knew what it was like to be in love and who took time to remove her boots and her jacket before going into the hallway; who paused to glance at her reflection in the oval gilt-edged mirror on the wall in the hall and smooth back her hair.

'Dandy, at last. I thought I heard a car.'

Anne spoke behind her from the arched entrance to the living room and Dandy turned to face her. Anne was looking as always pretty and elegant in a dress of printed silk, stripes of different greens decorated all over with white and dark green flowers. Her red-gold hair glowed softly in the lamplight.

'Jon is here,' she announced and coming across to Dandy hugged her and kissed her. 'I'm so glad you're back,' she whispered.

'I suppose you called him,' said Dandy.

'I did. I thought it best if you two met here,' explained Anne, looking troubled. 'His mother has been extremely unpleasant about the whole business. But I'm sure you and he can work something out if you're left alone, without interference. I'll leave you together. Morton is busy tonight preparing for the monthly board meeting tomorrow, so you can be sure you won't be interrupted.'

'You don't have to leave us alone,' Dandy protested. 'Anything we have to say to each other can be said when you're there. We don't have any secrets.'

'Oh, I think you do,' replied Anne. 'I'll be upstairs if you want me.'

Dandy hesitated for only a second before advancing into the living room. Light shone softly from well-placed, silk-shaded lamps and a log fire blazed in the fireplace. Under her feet the thick ivory-coloured broadloom was as soft as down. Jon was lounging on the big wide sofa in front of the fire, his blond hair shining, his long legs in fine mushroom-coloured corduroys stretched out before him. When he saw her he rose to his feet and looked at her with wary blue eyes.

'Hi, Jon,' Dandy said casually.

'Hi,' he muttered sullenly. Almost a year older than she was he looked younger. 'Why did you have to run away like that?' he demanded. 'We could have been in Martinique by now enjoying the water sports and soaking up the sunshine at the Club Med. if you hadn't taken off. You've really messed everything up, Dandy, as usual. What the hell got into you?'

'I had this vision on Thursday night of what marriage would be like for us and I decided I needed more time before taking the plunge,' she replied frankly.

'Then why didn't you tell me?' he grumbled, flinging himself down on the sofa.

'I had to be alone for a while, to sort my mind out.' She sat down on a nearby footstool. 'You didn't have to stay around you know. You could have gone to Martinique without me.'

'I wanted to go,' he replied bluntly, 'but my parents and yours said I'd better wait in Renwick in case you came back. I managed to change the flight reservation and the Club Med. people said we can arrive any time because the room is already paid for.' He leaned forward, staring into the fire, elbows on his knees, his chin cupped in his hands. 'So it's all arranged again,' he added woodenly. 'We can be married on Tuesday morning, thanks to the Rector being willing to fit us in then, and we can fly out in the afternoon.'

Dandy stared at him. His emotions had scarcely been touched by her running away. He hadn't really missed her at all and now he was assuming that because she had come back everything would go forward as planned. She drew a deep breath.

'You don't seem to understand, Jon,' she said quietly, hearing Yvan's voice urging her to come back and tell Jon to his face that she didn't want to marry him. 'I don't want to marry you, ever. And I wouldn't have come back today only . . . someone . . . I mean, I realised that it was only fair to tell you to your face that I've broken our engagement and to return this ring to you.'

She pulled the diamond ring off and handed it to him. That jolted him. He stared at the ring lying in the palm of her hand. Then he looked at her, his eyes puzzled.

'You're not serious,' he croaked.

'Yes, I am. Deadly serious. I don't want to marry you and I'm not going to marry you.'

'Why the hell not?' His face had gone red. 'What's wrong with me?'

'Nothing is wrong with you. You're a nice guy and I'm fond of you as if . . . as if you were my brother. Oh, why not face it Jon, we're not in love with each other. We don't turn each other on.'

'Since when has turning someone on been a reason for marriage?' he argued, frowning at her.

'Since the beginning of time,' she retorted. 'People who like being in bed together usually stay together.' She stared at him steadily, challenging him to disagree with her. 'You know that we've never experienced the slightest desire to make love with each other.'

He glanced away from her at the fire and chewed the corner of his lower lip and she guessed her challenge had hit its mark. Then he looked back at the ring.

'I'm fond of you too, Dandy,' he said. 'And I'm willing to try and make a go of marriage to you. I'm sure we could have fun together. We always have had fun when we've gone places together.'

'But don't you see? Being fond of a person,

having fun with her or with him isn't enough. There has to be something else,' Dandy argued intensely, her dark eyes burning with her conviction. 'There has to be an attraction you can't resist, a challenge you want to try and overcome for marriage to work, for two people to stay together forever. You and I have known each other too long. We know everything about each other. There's no mystery in our friendship, no excitement. Oh, I know I'm not putting this very well, but you must know what I mean. You feel it for that girl you've been seeing ... and sleeping with. The girl from Albany.'

His eyes went wide with shock and red colour suffused his face again.

'Who told you about Jenny?' he demanded hoarsely.

'It doesn't matter who told me. I know about her, that's all that matters.'

'And that's why you've decided to jilt me, I guess,' he exclaimed and than began to bluster. 'Look, Dandy, once you and I are married I'll stop seeing her. I swear I will.'

'But we're not going to be married. And knowing about Jenny isn't why I don't want to marry you. I just can't see myself making all those vows to you and keeping them for years and years, so why should I make them? I can't see myself living with you either. Now please will you take the ring back. You can offer it to Jenny. Maybe she would like to marry you.'

He took the ring from her, studied it for a moment then shoved it into his trouser pocket.

'Jenny is from the wrong side of the tracks as far as my parents are concerned,' he said with a touch

of bitterness. 'Her father used to work on the
railway before he was injured and had to go on
welfare and her mother works as a cleaner in the
State government buildings. Can you imagine my
parent's reactions if I took Jenny home with me
and told them I'd like to marry her?'

'Mmm. I can imagine,' said Dandy, nodding.
'So don't take her to see them . . . yet. Take her
with you to Martinique instead. You've said
yourself the tickets and room are all paid for. You
might as well make use of them, just take a
different woman with you.' An impish grin
hovered about her lips. 'A woman you like
sleeping with,' she added.

He stared at her in amazement and then began
to laugh.

'You really are something else,' he remarked.
'I've always known you're a rebel but I never
thought you'd incite anyone else to rebellion.' He
stood up and began to pace about the room
nervously. 'I wish I could do what you're telling
me I should do. I wish I had the courage to do it.'
He stopped in front of her, throwing out his hands
in a gesture of defeat. 'But you know my mother,'
he said. 'If I elope with Jenny, she'll never speak to
me again.'

'I know your mother,' replied Dandy with a
sigh. 'She's always dominated you, you being her
only son, and blond and blue-eyed into the
bargain, who could never, oh, never do anything
wrong.'

'Admitted,' he agreed also sighing. 'God, you've
no idea what she's like to live with.'

'Oh, yes I have. She's always tried to live your
life vicariously and she and I have already had

arguments about my so-called duties as a wife when I'm married to you. She went on at great length about your favourite foods and how I must be sure to have your clothes laid out for you to put on every morning, which shirts I should buy for you and so on and so on. Jon have you never done *anything* for yourself?'

'Not much,' he admitted with a self-mocking grin.

'Then it's time you started,' she snapped.

'But there's Dad, too,' he continued worriedly. 'He wants me to marry you. He said marriage to Morton's stepdaughter would be a good connection for me, help me along in my career with D.B.M.'

'And that's why you proposed?' gasped Dandy. 'The only reason you proposed?'

'I guess it is,' he admitted ruefully. 'You know how parents go on all the time about wanting you to be successful, about working hard and making the right contacts, about reaching the top of your profession? About getting established?'

'Yes, I know. I know only too well,' groaned Dandy. 'I've been through it too with Morton. How *we* feel and what *we* want doesn't seem to matter to our parents. It's what we can *achieve* that matters to them. They want *us* to be like *them*. Too bad if we know how to live and love and have more fun than they ever did. Oh, they make me tired.'

'So why did you do what your parents want and agree to marry me when I asked you?' said Jon shrewdly. 'Why didn't you rebel then?'

'I didn't want to make any more trouble for my mother. Whenever I do anything he doesn't like

Morton gets on to her,' muttered Dandy, rubbing the back of her head. It had begun to hurt again. 'I've been mixed up for years, not knowing what I am or where I should be going. All my girlfriends were either getting engaged or married so when you asked me I accepted, thinking I might feel better after I was married and that it would please Mother and Morton.' She smiled rather wanly at him. 'I'm sorry, Jon. I should never have said I would marry you. It was a mistake I made.'

'But I'm going to look such a fool,' he muttered, 'when everyone in this town and in the company finds out you've jilted me.'

'Then don't let it be known you've been jilted,' she suggested. 'Tell everyone that the decision not to marry each other was mutual and was reached after sensible discussion. That's what I'm going to say if anyone asks me why the marriage is off. We could even say we've been wise before the event, much wiser than our parents because we could see that marriage would be wrong for us.'

'Maybe you're right,' he murmured and gave her a quizzical glance. 'Is there someone else for you?' he asked. 'Like there is Jenny for me?'

'Yes, there is.'

'Good. I'm glad there is. I'm glad too that you had the courage to run away.' His expression was a little ashamed. 'You see I was having a hell of a time with my conscience. I didn't want to dump Jenny . . . but I didn't want to deceive you too. Thank God you're a rebel at heart, Dandy. We'd have both got into one hell of a mess if you weren't.'

'That's what I think too, but thanks for saying it Jon,' she replied, getting to her feet. 'It makes me feel a lot better to know there are no hard feelings between us. Still friends?'

'Still friends,' he said, smiling. 'I'll take myself off now.' He glanced at his watch.

'What time is she expecting you tonight?' she asked and he looked at her sharply, a tell-tale blush spreading across his fair-skinned face. When he saw she was smiling he smiled too.

'Around ten,' he said.

'So if you leave now you'll be right on time. I'll walk with you to the front door.'

When Jon had gone she wandered back to the living room and sat on the footstool again. Elbows on her knees she stared into the flames, seeing pictures in them; pictures of Yvan. He would be in Montreal by now. Where did he live? In a super-luxurious flat in one of the high-rise buildings near the river? Or did he live in a house? And did Niki, the woman he dreamed of, the woman he loved, live with him? If she did why hadn't she come with him to the cabin? Had they quarrelled? Was that why he had wanted to be alone for a few days?

'Where's Jon?'

Anne's voice interrupted her thoughts and she turned. Her mother was standing in the entrance to the room.

'He's gone,' Dandy replied.

'Already?' Anne advanced into the room and sat down in one of the high-back armchairs near the fire.

'He had a date.'

'So is all forgiven?' Anne asked. 'Are you and he going to be married on Tuesday? It's so good of the Rector to agree to perform the ceremony then. He could have refused to marry you after the way you've behaved. But he'll do anything for Morton.'

'Only because the Dyers have endowed the church of St Agnew with considerable amounts of money over the years,' muttered Dandy.

'Dandy, you mustn't say things like that,' Anne protested.

'Why not? It's the truth.'

'Maybe ... but ... well, it isn't always wise to come out with the truth, as I'm always telling you. You can be so easily misunderstood and so cause offence.'

'I'm sorry. I didn't mean to upset you,' Dandy said quietly. 'Yes, all is forgiven between Jon and me, but we're not getting married on Tuesday or on any other day.' She looked into the fire again, trying to see Yvan's profile in the flames. 'At least not to each other,' she added.

There was silence. Anne sat very still, her hands folded on her lap. At last she said in a low voice,

'Morton is going to be very angry when he knows.'

'So?' Dandy felt the antipathy she had always felt towards her stepfather flaring up. 'He has no right to be. My life is my own affair. I can do what I like, get married or not get married as I please. And the same goes for Jon. He doesn't have to marry me just because his parents want him to marry a woman with good connections. He isn't in love with me. He's in love with a girl from Albany. Let him marry her if he must be married.'

'How do you know about this girl?' Anne demanded.

'Sallyanne told me. She's seen them often,

walking around the Plaza, holding hands, smooching.' Dandy shrugged.

'So that's why you ran away on Friday.'

'No. Oh, I admit when I learned about Jenny I did wake up a bit, but knowing about her was only a contributory factor. I'd been thinking for some time I'd be a fool if I married Jon. But Morton has no right to be angry with me for changing my mind.'

'It isn't you he'll be angry with,' said Anne. 'He'll be angry with me.'

'Why? What have you done except encourage me to get married? It's not your fault I found out before it was too late that I don't want to be married to Jon. The blame is all mine.'

'Morton has always blamed me for you being the way you are and doing the things you do. He blamed me for your running away from that school. He blamed me when you went off to live with those hippies. He thinks I should have had more control over you and he thinks now that I should have stopped you from going away on Friday.'

'He shouldn't blame you and he's not going to this time,' asserted Dandy. 'He can be angry with me, say what he thinks of me to my face. I'll tell him myself that Jon and I aren't going to get married. But not tonight. Tomorrow. I feel too tired to cope with him tonight.'

She looked into the fire again. The flames had died down and there were no images of Yvan. Should she tell Anne about him? No. What had happened at the cabin in Vermont was her own special secret, something that had been shared only with him. She could never degrade it by telling a third party about it. It belonged only to her. and him.

'What are you going to do now that you've decided not to marry Jon?' asked Anne with a touch of weariness, as if she were tired of the whole matter.

'I've two week's holiday for the honeymoon, but I guess I'll take it and use the time to look around for another job. I've a yearning to go south or west, but I just might go north,' said Dandy. Yawning she rose to her feet and stretched her arms. 'Guess I'll go to my place and have some sleep,' she said.

'Dandy,' Jessie Perkins said there was a man staying at the cabin while you were there,' said Anne curiously. 'Did you go there to meet him?'

'No, I didn't. I didn't know he was there until I arrived on Friday night,' said Dandy, trying to sound casual. 'He's a friend of Gramps.'

'Oh. An older man,' murmured Anne, probably imagining someone like Gramps, in his mid-sixties.

'Yes, an older man,' repeated Dandy with a mocking twist of her lips. She bent and kissed Anne's cheek. 'Goodnight, Mom. I'll call in tomorrow to see you and don't forget, if Morton starts to criticise you because I'm not going to marry Jon, just refer him to me and tell him I'll pay the bills.'

Twenty minutes later, after walking up from the house by the river, Dandy unlocked the door of her small apartment in the big white house that had once been the rectory for the church. The apartment was just as she left it on Friday morning. In the kitchenette the remains of breakfast were still on the counter. In the bedroom the bed was still un-made. Nothing had changed.

But she had. She sank down on the crumpled bed. She had changed. She had fallen in love with a man who was not in love with her and this morning she had given herself to him and had let him penetrate to the core of her being; had let him possess not only her body but her soul too. But though they had been close and had been united in a beautiful explosion of joy, she had not possessed him in the way he had possessed her because he had kept his soul aloof from her.

And now she was here, alone again, and lonely, remembering and coveting his mouth, her body flooding with the heat of desire. Oh, what was she going to do now? What was she going to do?

The interview with her stepfather the next day wasn't pleasant but she finally succeeded in convincing him that he mustn't blame Anne for anything she had done and also to accept her decision not to marry Jon. He grumbled a lot until she told him she would pay for her wedding dress, the cake and the flowers that had been ordered and delivered, and she left him feeling that at last he realised she was off his hands, no longer his responsibility.

Later the same day when she was sitting at her desk at the apartment trying to compose a letter of application for a job she had found advertised in another part of the country, the phone rang. The caller was her friend Sallyanne Porter.

'I've just heard that you're back in town,' said Sallyanne. 'Supposing I pick up some Kentucky fried chicken and bring it round and you can tell me what you've been up to over the weekend?'

'Sounds great,' said Dandy.

Fifteen minutes later Sallyanne arrived carrying a cardboard bucket containing fried chicken and french fries. Blonde and blue-eyed she teeterred in her high-heeled boots into the kitchen and set the food out on plates which she carried into the living room where Dandy was still typing.

'What are you doing?' asked Sallyanne, putting the plates down on the coffee table and curling up on the sofa.

'Applying for a job in California,' replied Dandy.

'You're leaving D.B.M.?' squeaked Sallyanne.

'Maybe. If I can get a job some place else.' Dandy flopped down beside her friend.

'I guess your stepfather asked you to leave, I hear he was pretty mad at you when you ran away.'

'No, he hasn't asked me to leave. I decided it's time I got out of Renwick. Have you seen anything of Jon, today?'

'No. But that's what I called round to tell you. He's moved out from his parent's place, and Mrs Van Fleet is in hospital with a nervous breakdown. It seems that Jon didn't go back home last night after seeing you and he phoned his folks this morning to tell them he wouldn't be getting married to you tomorrow either but that he'd be flying to Martinique as arranged only he'd be taking someone else with him.' Sallyanne paused for breath then added, 'I think it's so romantic, don't you?'

'What is?'

'He and Jenny going off together tomorrow, eloping.'

'If I'd have thought that going off anywhere

with Jon was romantic I'd have married him, wouldn't I?' said Dandy dryly.

'I guess so,' sighed Sallyanne. 'How long do you think it will take you to find another job? Supposing you don't, what will you do?'

'Stay on at D.B.M. I guess. But I'm not worried. Something will turn up,' said Dandy optimistically.

But nothing had turned up by the end of her holiday and so she returned to work in the computer programming department. A few days later Anne and Morton left for Europe on a business-combined-with-pleasure trip that was to last for two months. When they had gone Dandy breathed a sigh of relief. Now she could do what she liked without having to take into account how her behaviour would affect Anne's relationship with Morton.

Two weeks dragged by. She heard nothing in reply to the applications she had made for jobs in other parts of the country. She began to feel very depressed and the weather didn't help. Winter seemed to have extended itself right into the month of April, and in spite of the fact that buds were blurring the branches of the trees there was still ice in the river and still snow on the tops of the mountains.

She was sitting at her desk one evening typing out yet another letter of application for a job she had just found advertised when the apartment door, which she usually left unlocked when she was at home in the daytime, opened and Douglas Kerr walked in and started talking to her as if he hadn't been away for nearly five months.

'Hey, what's going on?' he grumbled, his dark

brown eyes twinkling at her from under their thick
eyebrows. 'I called at the house to see Anne and
Morton and found it shut up. No one there, yet
I'm sure I wrote and told Anne I'd be arriving
today.'

'Oh, Gramps, it's good to see you,' gasped
Dandy, running over to him and hugging him.
'Mom and Morton have gone to Europe and from
there they're going to Japan and Australia.
Business as well as pleasure. You know Morton,
he feels guilty if he has a holiday so he has to
arrange to meet customers in various places and
do a sales pitch for D.B.M.'

'So where am I going to stay the night?' he
asked.

'You can stay here, if you don't mind sleeping
on a hideabed.'

'Is this it?' Douglas asked, kicking the sofa with
a booted foot. Tall and rangy he didn't look his
age of sixty-five because his black hair was only
slightly sprinkled with grey and his face was
healthily tanned.

'It's really quite comfortable and I'll make it up
like a real bed,' said Dandy persuasively.

'I thought you were married now,' he shot the
question at her.

'No. I changed my mind. I'll tell you all about it
if you'd like to take me out to dinner.'

'I'll take you out, but not dressed like that.
You'll have to put a skirt on.'

'Okay,' said Dandy, with a grin. 'There's a
good Austrian restaurant over in Catskill if you
like veal and apple strudel. Want me to phone and
book us a table?'

'Might be a good idea.'

An hour later they were sitting at a table in the restaurant which was tucked away down a side street in Catskill, and were being waited on by a smiling waitress. Austrian walzes played continuously over a loud-speaker and while they drank beer from big steins as they waited for the food Dandy told Douglas all that had happened since he had left New York, beginning with Jon's proposal of marriage and ending with her return from Vermont to the Dyer house.

'Well, I'm surprised you let yourself be persuaded to marry young Jon and that you let it go on so long,' he remarked critically.

'It might not have happened if you hadn't gone away,' she retorted. 'And I was trying to please Mom and Morton, I really was.'

'Then let it be a lesson to you,' he growled at her. 'How were things in Vermont? Cabin okay?'

'Except for the generator. It had broken down when I arrived but Yvan fixed it the next day.'

The waitress arrived with the main course and she sat back to watch her grandfather's face for his reaction to her mention of Yvan. His eyebrows shot up in surprise.

'Yvan Rambert?' he said.

'Is there any other Yvan in your life?' she asked with a grin. 'He's a Frenchman who lives in Montreal and is a Canadian citizen now. He said he'd met you at Stowe, that time you broke your leg, and that you'd kept in touch with him ever since.'

'That's right. So he was in the cabin when you arrived. Anyone with him?'

'No. He was waiting for me in the dark—there

was no light you see, the generator having broken down.' Dandy gave a laugh. 'He thought I was breaking in and I thought he had broken in. I tried out my karate on him. But I didn't stand a chance.'

'I wish I'd been there,' Douglas's eyes narrowed shrewdly as he watched a wild rose colour flush Dandy's face. It was the first time he had ever seen her blush. 'Did you like Yvan?'

'Not at first, but he sort of grew on me,' said Dandy as lightly as she could. 'You wouldn't know his address in Montreal would you? I was thinking of driving up there next week and I'd like to see him again.'

'I have his address somewhere,' said Douglas vaguely. 'Yes, we met about two years ago at Stowe. He had a lovely woman with him, a fellow countrywoman of his who was also working in Montreal for an advertising agency. They had something pretty powerful going between them.' He looked across at her again. Some of the colour had faded from her cheeks and her lips had compressed.

'You mean they were lovers?' she said.

'That's what I mean.'

'What was her name?' Dandy laid down her fork. The good food was suddenly tasteless.

'Darned if I can remember,' replied Douglas. He was eating as if he hadn't had a good meal in months.

'Could it have been Niki?'

'Mmm. I think that was it. Did he tell you about her?'

'Not really. He told me very little about himself and every time I tried to find out more he would close up like a clam. Oh, he was very cool and sophisticated, yet I had this feeling, Gramps, that underneath he was boiling . . . like a volcano about to erupt.'

'Aha.' Douglas's eyes twinkled knowingly. 'Sounds to me as if you got his measure. Takes a rebel to recognise another rebel, I guess, and Yvan has done his share of rebelling, just like you have.'

'Tell me about him,' Dandy urged.

'Well, he's the only son of a French General. General Gilles Rambert, to be exact, *Croix de Guerre* and all that. Yvan was supposed to go into the army like his father before him and all the other Ramberts. But he refused. Dug his heels in and left home to get a job with a civil engineering company as a draughtsman and then later took a degree in engineering.'

'Why did he come to Canada?'

'He told me it was a spirit of adventure. He just wanted to see what was on the other side of the Atlantic Ocean. What he didn't tell me was that before he left France he was involved in a scandal.'

'If he didn't tell you, how do you know?'

'I made it my business to find out about him when I was in Paris. I visited an old friend of mine who used to work for the French Embassy in Washington and asked him about the Rambert family, in particular about General Rambert's son.'

'Well, go on, go on,' urged Dandy impatiently. 'What did he tell you about Yvan?'

'It seems that Yvan had an affair with the wife of a civil servant who was responsible for handing out government contracts to private companies and he managed to persuade the woman to influence her husband into giving a big contract to the company Yvan was working for at the time.' Douglas paused dramatically. 'He was found out,' he added dryly. 'The ensuing publicity put an end to his career with the company and also caused him to quarrel, yet again, with his father. So he left France.'

'A black sheep,' remarked Dandy softly. 'Oh, I knew it. I guessed there was something in him that was like me. And I love him all the more for it.'

'Did you say "love"?' queried Douglas.

'Yes, I love him. I fell in love with him that weekend and as soon as I can I'm going to Montreal to see him.'

'He's invited you?'

'No, but I'm going just the same. I have to. These past few weeks without seeing him have been awful. If I don't go to see him I'll go crazy.'

'Dandy, listen to me,' said Douglas sharply. 'You're not going to see Yvan if he hasn't invited you.'

'Why not?'

'Because he wouldn't like it if you appeared at his door uninvited.'

'How do you know?'

'I think I'm a pretty good judge of character and I believe Yvan would have no time for any woman who chased after him. Don't run after him, Dandy,' he advised quietly. 'You'll only get hurt if you do. He's in love with Niki.'

'Then why wasn't she with him at the cabin? And why did he . . . I mean how could he . . .?' She broke off. She couldn't possibly admit to her grandfather that she and Yvan had made love together at the cabin. To do that would embarrass both him and herself.

'Perhaps she couldn't come with him. Perhaps she was away. I got the impression the one time I met her that she was very interested in her career. She could have gone abroad, maybe back to France for some reason.' He smiled at her. 'People who are lovers don't have to be together all the time, you know.'

'I guess not,' she muttered and sighed. 'Oh, I suppose I might as well forget him. Did I tell you I'm looking around for another job? I think it's time I left D.B.M. and got out of Renwick. I'm really finding the place dreary and constraining.'

'Not a bad idea,' he agreed. 'Time you spread your wings and took off.'

There was no more talk about Yvan, and next morning Douglas left early, eager to get to Vermont and to start writing his next novel. It wasn't until later that Dandy realised he had not given her Yvan's address in Montreal. At first she was irritated with herself for not reminding him to give it to her, but after a while she decided it was for the best. It was best if she didn't know where Yvan lived. If she knew his address she would always be tempted to drive up to Montreal to see him and would risk being hurt by him more than she had been already.

But was she still in love with him? If she could see him again she might find out if her feelings for him were true love or just a passing fancy. She was haunted by him and spent many hours remembering how he looked, recalling their conversations and, worst of all, indulging in erotic memories until she ached with the desire to feel again the pressure of his lips against hers and the touch of his fingertips on her skin.

The slow change of season from winter to spring aggravated her physical yearnings, as melting snow on the hills swelled small streams and ice cracked everywhere. Everything was preparing to burst out into new growth and so it was with her, she thought, one beautiful calm evening at the beginning of May as she let herself into the apartment after having been to the local cinema with Sallyanne. Like the sap in the trees her blood was rising, boiling through her veins so that she felt swollen with desire and longed to be with Yvan.

It was going to be one of those tormenting nights when she would toss and turn wondering what to do next, wondering where to go. What was the use of going to bed? She might as well stay up, watch the late movie on TV, drink some beer, smoke some cigarettes in an effort to numb her mind. Oh, God, was this what her life was going to be like forever more?

In the bedroom she stripped and pulled on a nightshirt made from cotton poplin, navy and red overcheck on white, which was really an extended version of a well-tailored shirt made by a superior shirt company. It clung to her breasts and revealed her legs, but she wasn't concerned about her appearance and didn't care that the shirt emphasised all that was feminine about her. After all there was no one there to see her.

She was just going through to the kitchenette to take a beer from the fridge when the doorbell rang. She went into the living room and over to the door of the apartment. Her hand on the latch she hesitated. There had been a number of robberies with violence as well as a couple of muggings and a rape in Renwick recently and all the victims had been women who lived alone. Leaving the chain in its slot she opened the door and looked through the gap between the edge of the door and the jamb.

For a brief hectic moment she wondered if she was hallucinating as she stared incredulously at the man who was standing outside the door.

'Yvan?' she asked cautiously.

'Hello, Dandy.' His lips quirked into a smile. 'I have just got here. May I come in?'

CHAPTER SIX

No, it couldn't be Yvan. He couldn't have come to her because he didn't know where she lived. He wasn't really there. She was going out of her mind and was imagining he was there. She closed her eyes, shutting out his image, and began to close the door but it wouldn't close. Something was stopping it. Opening her eyes she looked down. A foot encased in an elegant tan-coloured boot was wedged between the door and the jamb. Pale avocado green corduroy slanted over the boot.

'Dandy.' Amusement roughened his voice. 'You have to take the chain off before you can open the door properly and before I can come in. That is if you really want me to come in.'

She looked up. He was there, all right, his light eyes shimmering with blue light, his lips curling in derision.

'Oh, yes, yes. I want you to come in,' she croaked.

With a shaking hand she slid the chain out of the slot. Her heart was racing with excitement and her cheeks were suddenly burning.

'Please come in,' she invited and pulled the door open wide. 'It was just that I never expected to see you of all people here, actually here at my door and I wondered if my mind had flipped.'

She realised she was babbling incoherently and that he had stepped past her into the living room so that she was talking to the space where he had

116

been standing outside the door and the door was still open. She shut it, slid the chain into the slot and turned, leaning back against the door for support, fully expecting to find the room empty because he had vanished into thin air.

But he was there, standing in the middle of the room, his hands in the slit pockets of his wide shouldered suede jacket which had knitted ribbed waistband, wristbands and collar and which zipped up the front and he looked cool and sophisticated as usual. He glanced around the room curiously and she wished suddenly and vehemently that she had tidied it up when she had come in from the movies. He must think she was a slob, a messy, careless slob.

'How did you know I live here?' she asked, rushing across the room and picking up the tray on which the remains of her TV dinner had dried, and which was still on the coffee table.

'It was easy,' he replied following her into the kitchenette and watching her dump dirty dishes in the sink and turn on the taps. 'I remember the name of the town where you say you live. I look for it on the road map and I drive down here. Once I am here I look you up in the telephone directory.' He shrugged and made a gesture with one hand.

He unzipped his jacket. Under it he was wearing a checked shirt in two greens. His elegance made her uncomfortably aware of the casualness of her own attire, of the thin poplin nightshirt which showed so much leg, of her bare feet, of the wild tangle of her long hair, falling forward over her shoulders and half covering her face. With a movement of entirely unconscious femininity she swept two long swatches of hair back behind her shoulders. His eyes followed her movements.

'Have you had dinner?' she asked politely, trying to remember the contents of the fridge. There was nothing in it, nothing at all she could offer to him whose cooking was so superior to her own. In every way she was at a disadvantage.

'Yes. At Jack's in Albany. It's a good restaurant.'

'One of the best,' she replied with relief. 'Then would you like a drink? I have beer, Coke, or coffee.'

'Beer would be good,' he said. He was looking amused again, as if her efforts to offer him hospitality caused him much secret laughter. No doubt he was accustomed to being made welcome by women who were carefully dressed and coiffured. He would be used to Niki greeting him in a long slinky dress and offering him wine, she thought miserably.

She opened the fridge and took out two bottles of beer. She put the bottles on the counter and found an opener. She had always believed herself to be pretty competent at opening beer and soda bottles but her hands were still shaking so much she couldn't get the opener to grip on the fluted edges of a bottle cap.

He stepped over until he was beside her. His hand closed on both of hers and lifted them away from the bottle. Then he took both her hands in both of his so that her palms were resting on his palms. He studied her fingers.

'You are not wearing the diamond ring,' he said. 'Does that mean you gave it back to Jon?' He looked up and right into her eyes. Her knees shook and a longing to lean against him swept through her.

'Yes.' His hands shifted to her wrists and his thumbs moved over them in a subtle caress. Her pulses throbbed in response. 'I gave it back to him the night I came back to Renwick. And it was all right. He didn't really want to marry me either. He's going to marry someone else, I think.'

'Good. So now you are really free to do what you want,' he murmured.

'Yes, I'm really free now,' she whispered.

'I'll open the beer,' he said coolly, dropping her hands. 'Do you have any glasses?'

She showed him where the glasses were and hurried into the living room to plump up cushions, fold newspapers and push them away with the magazines that were scattered about the place. She drew the drapes, something she hardly ever did, and switched off the ceiling light so that light came only from the big pottery table lamp that stood on a small occasional table near the window. She thought the room looked better, still casual and contemporary, but more romantic.

Yvan sat on the sofa and she sat on one of the big floor cushions. He lifted his glass to her in a silent toast and drank some beer. Dandy drank too. Questions were bubbling up inside her but she wasn't going to ask them. She wasn't going to risk offending him. He had come to her, unexpectedly, and he had brought with him that crackling excitement. Already she was aflame with desire to be closer to him but she wasn't going to say anything in case he walked out and left her again.

'So what have you been doing here since you come back, since you do not get married to Jon?' he asked.

He was speaking English awkwardly, confusing the tenses, leaving out some words, she noticed, as if he too were excited by this meeting.

'I'm looking for another job in another place,' she said.

'You have left D.B.M.?'

'Not yet, but I will one day. But what about you? What have you been doing?'

'Working on the design of a dam that is to be built in a South American country. If my company gets the contract I might be sent out there to be the project engineer and supervise the construction.'

He was staring at something. She followed the direction of his gaze. He was staring at her knees and thighs. The nightshirt had ridden up exposing them. She shifted, trying to ease the skirt of the nightgown down and managed to slop beer from her glass on to her legs. Reaching forward he took the glass from her and set it with his own on the coffee table.

'Come and sit beside me,' he invited. 'You are too far away.'

Dandy obeyed and sank down on the sofa beside him, thinking how uncomfortable it was. She had acquired it from her mother. Anne had had no use for it for years and it had been stored in the basement of the Dyer house. Now a spring in the sofa poked up into one of her buttocks. Curling her legs under her, she sat up straight, trying not to lean towards Yvan in case he thought she was making up to him.

'Would you like that, to be sent to South America I mean?' she asked stiffly, thinking they were talking to each other as if they had only just met and had never been intimate.

'Yes, I would.' He turned towards her and stretched an arm along the back of the sofa. Taking hold of a tress of her hair he began to play with it, twisting it round his fingers. With a finger of his other hand he flicked the collar of her nightshirt. 'I like this gown,' he murmured.

His finger slid inside the unbuttoned opening of the shirt and moved downwards, the fingernail digging delicately into her skin as it traced a breathtaking line to the deep cleft between her breasts. She turned to look at him, her lips parting on a gasp of pleasure.

'It is, the gown, as you would say ... sexy,' he whispered. 'It is not at all like that other thing you wore at the cabin.'

Their eyes on the same level they stared at each other, feasting on each other's appearance. Slowly their heads tipped forward and their eyelids drooped over their eyes as they looked at each other's lips. Yet still they did not kiss.

'Why have you come to see me?' whispered Dandy.

'I was curious. I wanted to find out if you had married Jon or not.'

'I might not have been here. I might have gone away,' she murmured.

'But you haven't gone away. You're here and I would like to kiss you. Would you like for me to kiss you, Dandy?' he said softly.

'Yes. Please.'

She lifted her parted lips willingly to his and her breath rushed out in a sigh of capitulation as his mouth covered hers. Her lips moved in response to the subtle stroking of his and then his tongue, hot with passion, was confronting hers, sending a forceful demanding message along her nerves, heating her up, melting her.

Then suddenly he had gone, had withdrawn from her completely. She opened her eyes and saw his, blue-grey between black lashes, dancing with laughter.

'That was nice. It was worth coming for,' he said. 'I've thought much about you, these past few weeks.'

'I've thought of you, often,' she admitted too, wishing he would kiss her again. 'But I didn't think ... well, what I'm trying to say is ... I thought you wouldn't remember me. I thought you'd forget me.'

A shadow seemed to flit across his face and his eyelids drooped over his eyes. His lips twisted in a cynical grimace.

'I'm not surprised you thought that,' he said. 'I'm not surprised you believe me to be the sort of man who takes what he wants from a woman and then forgets her, because I have done that ... in the past.' He looked at her, his eyes sombre now. 'But the other women haven't been innocents like you and it has bothered me that I broke one of my own rules of behaviour while I was with you. I allowed myself to seduce a virgin. . . .'

'No, no. I won't have that. You didn't seduce me,' she argued. 'What happened between us happened because I wanted it to happen and afterwards I didn't feel outraged or ashamed, or anything like that. I was just glad that I'd been with you, glad that it had happened for me with someone who can make love like you do.' She touched his cheek with shy fingers. 'But I'm glad too, that you remembered me and have come to see me. Will you stay the night here, with me?'

His eyes began to dance again and the shadow was chased from his face by the elusive glimmer of his smile.

'I was hoping you would invite me to stay,' he said, gathering her against him and rubbing his cheek against hers. His tongue tickled her ear, then his teeth bit the lobe sending exquisite tingles along her nerves. 'But I must know first if you have a bedroom with a good bed in it,' he added mockingly, 'I have no wish to make love with you or to sleep with you on this damnably uncomfortable sofa.'

'It is lumpy, isn't it?' Her laugh was a warm gurgle of sound. 'But there is a bedroom, with a double bed ... but....' She pushed free of him and sprang to her feet. 'I haven't made the bed yet. You mustn't come in there until I've made it. Promise?'

'I promise,' he said laughing too as he stood up. 'I'll go and fetch my bag from the car.' He kissed her again, a flagrantly erotic kiss which rocked her where she stood even though he didn't touch her anywhere else. 'I'll be with you soon, my love,' he whispered. 'In the best possible way.'

He left the apartment and Dandy went into action, dancing across the living room and into the bedroom, pirouetting with joy.

He had come and he wanted her. He had come without being invited to kiss her and to sleep with her. For one whole night he would be here and beyond that she didn't want to know. Tonight was all that mattered. Tonight they would love lavishly until they were exhausted and then would sleep in each other's arms. Tomorrow could take care of itself. There was no yesterday, no tomorrow, only tonight.

She stripped the bed and put clean sheets on it. When it was made she hurried about tidying the room, aware that Yvan had returned to the apartment and was taking a shower. She pushed discarded clothing into the clothes closet and shut its door, then gave the room a quick critical glance. The bedside lamp cast golden light across the bed. The shadows in the rest of the room were mysteriously purple. All that was missing was soft music and perhaps a bottle of wine, preferably champagne, to celebrate the coming of Yvan to her.

Laughing at her own romantic fantasy she caught sight of her reflection in the long mirror on the front of the clothes closet door and laughter gave way to a scowl of irritation. Why didn't her outward appearance express how she felt? Why didn't she look like the passionate woman she was? Why did she look like a tomboy even though her figure was softly rounded and her hair was long, like a black cloak?

As she stared a figure appeared behind her in the mirror; the glimmer of a pale face under damp black hair, the shimmer of blue-grey eyes, the soft sheen of a blue velvet dressing gown crossing a bare chest sprinkled with black hairs. Yvan came right up behind her. He put his hands on her shoulders and against the side of her throat his lips burned. When he lifted his head his glance met hers in the mirror.

Slowly his hands slid forward and over her breasts, pressing them briefly and tantalisingly before his fingers began to flick undone the buttons of her nightshirt. Gently he stroked the open shirt away from her body, revealing it to her own fascinated gaze.

'You see how beautiful you are, how pure and white,' he whispered as the nightshirt fell to the floor. 'You see now why I had to come and *see* you again? It was to make sure you are as I remembered you.'

Deftly he spun her round and the soft velvet of his robe added its own titillation to her skin.

'I like your body,' he continued. 'I like what it does to mine.'

Lifting her he carried her to the bed. In the lamplight his skin had a golden sheen, the muscles rippling under it as he shed his robe and lay down beside her. He was scented with her lavender soap and in the yellow glow from the lamp his eyes took on a lavender hue, growing bigger as they came closer to hers, until she could see only one, until his lips were devouring hers again.

Her eyes closing she whirled out of control in a delirium of sensuous delight. Shifting and twisting against him she smoothed and stroked him, seeking and finding new hollows, tantalising him until with a tortured groan he pushed her on to her back.

'I like this best of all,' he said breathlessly. 'I like the feel of you under me, soft as down yet warm and pulsing with life.'

Unable to find words in English he continued in French, and as his passion burst beyond control he flooded her with his essence sweeping her out and up to a crest of sensation from which she floated down and down, round and round to the reality of the tumble bed, the moist warmth of their skins, the thudding of their hearts.

They lay in silence, his legs sprawled across hers, his face in her hair. Her hands lay lax against his back. After a while his weight became dead and she guessed he had fallen asleep, so moving cautiously she reached out, found a blanket and pulled it up over them.

She closed her eyes hoping to fall asleep too, but as the aftermath of ecstasy wore off cold reason took its place. He had come to her but only to use her body for his own pleasure. He had pleasured her too, but only so that his own satisfaction could be greater. He didn't love her as she wanted to be loved.

Regret for having let him stay the night swept through her like a raw cutting wind. She tried to get from under him, pushing at him until he woke up and rolled away from her, taking most of the blanket with him and curling up on his side, his back to her.

'I wish you hadn't come,' she said and hit at his broad back with her fist. He turned over to face her.

'What did you say?' he asked. He saw the tears brimming in her eyes and leaned over her. 'Ah, Dandy, what is the matter? Why do you cry. Wasn't it good for you? I thought it was as good for you as it was for me, that it was perfect.'

'I still wish you hadn't come. I would have gotten over it if you hadn't come,' she insisted.

'But you said. . . .' He broke off and drew a harsh impatient breath. 'So, if that is how you feel I will go away now,' he said coolly and moved away from her. She opened her eyes quickly. He was sitting on the side of the bed and was reaching for his robe. She flung herself after him, winding her arms about him.

'No, no. That isn't what I meant to say. Oh, why does everything come out the wrong way?' She leaned her head against his back. 'What I meant was I wish you hadn't come beacuse I'll hurt so much when you go away again and after . . . after what we've done tonight I don't think I'll be able to bear it if you . . . if you leave me again.'

'And is that all?' he queried, turning to her. 'Is that the only reason you are crying?'

'Isn't it enough?'

'It is enough,' he replied gravely, although a muscle quivered at one corner of his mouth as if he was having difficulty in controlling his amusement. 'And there is no need for you to cry. You can come with me when I leave here, if you wish.'

'Come with you?' She sat up and stared at him. 'You mean you'd like me to go back with you to Montreal?'

'That is what I would like, yes.'

'To live with you there?'

'To live with me there.' Again there was a glint of amusement in his face.

'I. . . .' she began and stopped, to glance at him suspiciously. 'But I'm not your kept woman,' she blurted suddenly. 'And I refuse to be.'

'Would you refuse to be my wife?' he asked softly, stroking one of her bare thighs suggestively, all the time holding her gaze with his.

'Pardon me,' she whispered in bewilderment. 'Did you say "wife"?'

'I did. Would you like to go with me to Montreal and marry me there? Doesn't that appeal to your rebel heart?'

It did of course. She could think of nothing more romantic than running away with him over the border to be married in Montreal. She couldn't refuse.

'When would we go?' she asked, shy of the way he was looking at her, confused by the touch of his hand on her thigh, her brain beginning to reel a little from the sensuousness that was being transmitted from his fingertips.

'Tomorrow, if you can. I have to go back tomorrow to be at work on Monday.'

'I . . . I'm not sure if I can go,' she muttered, moving away from him and curling her legs under her, trying to separate herself from him so that she could think more clearly, resenting a little the power he could exert over her. He knew he could defeat her by making love to her. 'I have to know first why you want to marry me,' she said, wanting to know really what had happened to Niki, the woman he was in love with but afraid to ask him in case he snarled at her. 'I hope it isn't because you feel you ought to marry me because of what happened at the cabin. I told you then you don't have to feel responsible for me.'

'But that isn't why I want to marry you,' he said quietly and began to pull the bedclothes away from her. 'I want to marry you so that I have the right to insist you live with me all the time, so that I can take you to bed with me whenever I wish, so that I can introduce you to my friends and family as my wife rather than as . . .' again his lips twitched with mocking humour, 'than as my kept woman,' he finished.

'And those are the only reasons?'

'They are the only reasons. But if they are not enough we'll forget the whole idea of marriage and I'll go back to Montreal without you. I do not want a reluctant, suspicious wife,' he said coldly.

'You mean you won't let me go with you to Montreal if I won't agree to marry you?' she asked in surprise.

'I mean exactly that.' The tone of his voice was icy. He seemed to be getting to the end of his patience.

'Do I have to decide now?' she asked, miserably aware he was withdrawing from her again yet there was still so much she wanted to know. She wanted to know about Niki and why he didn't want to marry the woman.

'Now,' he retorted. 'And perhaps this will help you to make up your mind. If you agree to marry me I'll stay the rest of the night with you and we'll leave together tomorrow for Montreal. If you refuse to marry me then we'll say goodbye and I'll leave by myself now and will never come back.'

'Oh, no, no. Please don't go without me. I want to go with you. I want to be with you forever and ever.' She flung her arms around him again to prevent him from leaving the bed.

'Forever is a long time,' he said dryly, but he began to stroke her hair. 'Does that mean you promise to marry me when we get to Montreal?'

'Yes, I'll marry you because I prefer to be introduced to your friends and family as your wife rather than as your kept woman,' she whispered.

'Where's the difference?' he taunted, deliberately aggravating her. 'All wives are kept women.'

She started to argue with him, taking exception to this expression of male chauvinism, and he loomed over her, his attitude threatening.

'I can see there is only one way for me to deal with an argumentative rebel like you,' he growled.

'And that is?' she challenged.

'To stop you like this,' he whispered.

He kissed her again, melting her resistance with the heat of his passion until once again they became fused together in an act of indescribable erotic pleasure so that later, when she lay in drowsy contentment, curled up against him, Dandy had to admit to herself reluctantly that his great attraction for her lay in his ability to overwhelm her with his superior strength and determination to get what he wanted. He was more than her match, he was her master, and while he was willing to show he could dominate her by making love to her she would always be his even though she knew he didn't love her in the way he loved Niki. For not once during the night had he said to her *I love you, I love you very much* as he had murmured in his sleep to the woman of his dreams.

The sun was high in the sky next morning when he woke her, his voice edged with the crispness of authority.

'If you really want to go to Montreal with me today you will get up and get ready. There is much for you to do before you can leave.'

She sat up in bed and swept her hair back. He was already dressed and shaved. Hands in the pockets of his corduroys he stood beside the bed and looked at her coldly. He was her lover and she had promised to marry him and yet she didn't know him. Always he withdrew from her like this, behind a steel door.

'I've made coffee and breakfast. Can you be ready to leave here by two this afternoon?'

'Yes, I can. All I have to do is tell the landlord I'm leaving. The rent is paid until the end of May. I'll write a note and put the key in it and put it in his mail box in the hallway.'

'And your mother and stepfather. Do we have to go and see them?'

'No, they're away, right now. There's only Gramps.' She chewed at her lip. What would her grandfather say when he heard that Yvan had come to her instead of her having to go to him? 'But I can't tell him either because he doesn't have a phone at the cabin. I know, I'll write to them all from Montreal after we're married.'

'You are sure you wouldn't prefer to wait until your parents return fom their trip?' he asked. 'Perhaps you would like them to be present when we marry?'

'But they won't be back until the beginning of June and I don't think I can wait that long, not now that you've asked me. Can you?'

'I wouldn't be urging you now to get ready to come with me this afternoon if I wanted to wait,' he replied softly, sitting down on the side of the bed and leaning towards her, his eyes blazing suddenly with desire. 'I want you, Dandy, very much. I want you to come with me today.'

They left soon after noon in separate cars, Dandy having decided she would like to have hers with her and drove in the soft spring sunlight along the Northway through the New York countryside past thick woods misted with thousands of swollen pink woods and into the fertile plains of the province of Quebec. Along the south shore of the St Lawrence River they drove with the

city on their right, twinkling with many lights in
the dusk. Over the Mercier Bridge and down
another fast road that took them to a suburb
beside Lake St Louis and a street of modern town
houses in an exclusive residential area, one of
which belonged to Yvan.

'I bought it last December,' he explained in
answer to Dandy's question about how long he
had lived in it. They were carrying her luggage into
the hallway at the time. 'You see, I was . . . .' He
broke off as the telephone bell rang. 'Excuse me,'
he murmured and went on into the living room of
the house and in a few seconds she heard him
speaking in French to whoever had called him.

Sometimes, in the days that followed, as they
prepared for the civil marriage ceremony, she
often wondered what he had been going to tell her
when the phone had rung and had interrupted
him. Had he been going to tell her why he had
bought the house? Had he bought it to live in it
with Niki? She knew that she ought to ask him
what had happened to Niki and why he had
decided to marry herself instead of the woman of
his dreams. She supposed she should know
everything about him before making the final
commitment to him, but she still hesitated about
asking him personal questions. And then, she
would argue, if he wanted her to know he would
tell her himself, wouldn't he? And it would be best
if he told her without her asking him.

Besides she was too happy being with him and
she didn't want to spoil that happiness, so she
didn't ask any questions about Niki. But she did
ask him if any of his family would be present when
they were finally married in the local town hall.

'No. There is only my sister, Jacqueline, and my father and they are both in France. They live in Normandy,' he replied. 'They will be coming over later, in the summer to visit me.' His mouth twisted a little. 'My father and I do not get on with each other and I would like my marriage to you to be a *fait accompli* before he comes.'

'Why don't you get on with him?'

'That is a difficult question to answer,' he said with a laugh. 'Probably the answer lies in our characters. And then there is a big age gap between us. He didn't marry my mother until he was forty and he was forty-four when I was born, a gap of two generations, not just one. He'll be seventy-five this year.'

'Old enough to be your grandfather. How old was your mother when they married?'

'About the same age that you are now. It was an arranged marriage. She was the daughter of one of his fellow generals in the French army.'

'Another big age difference,' she remarked, pleased that at last he was telling her something about himself, or at least about his family. Maybe he might tell her about Niki too, if she was careful and didn't ask too many questions. 'How old is your sister?'

'Jackie is younger than I am by two years. She is married and has two children, a boy and a girl, but I haven't seen them because I haven't been back to France since I left and she has never come here. This summer she will come to accompany my father who has stated a wish to see me before he dies.' His mouth twisted sardonically and he added quietly, 'My mother's death had a bad effect on my father. He seemed to withdraw into himself.

Although he carried on with his career in the army he withdrew from the rest of life, from his responsibility for Jackie and me. When we weren't in a private school he left us in the care of various housekeepers. I don't know about Jackie, but I grew up resenting his lack of interest in us and with little respect for his opinions or his authority. You understand?'

'Yes, I understand very well,' she said thinking of herself and Morton.

'Every time we met we clashed,' Yvan went on. 'And when I was eighteen and ready to leave school he arranged for me to go into the army. I refused. And I left home. I went to work for an engineering company owned by the husband of my mother's sister, Cécile. My father was furious with me and for a long time we didn't meet. When we did, we quarrelled again and soon afterwards I came to Canada.'

'What did you quarrel about?' asked Dandy.

'Everything and nothing,' he replied with a shrug, 'but mostly about my refusal to marry a woman he had chosen to be my wife. He told me to leave his house and never to go back. I never have been back.' He paused, frowning then went on slowly, 'But last year my sister wrote and said he had been ill and wished very much to see me so I invited them both to come here.' He turned to her smiling and stroked her cheek. 'They will come in the summertime and they will meet you, my wife,' he said softly.

'Your father might not like me,' murmured Dandy, leaning towards him, hoping he would kiss her and that they would spend the rest of the evening making love.

'Will it matter to you if he does or doesn't like you?' he demanded, with a flash of jealousy. 'I thought I am the most important man in your life.'

'Oh, you are, you are,' she whispered, winding her arms about his neck. 'And it won't matter if he doesn't like me as long as you do.' And after that there were no more questions.

They were married on a bright windy May day and spent a week's honeymoon in a cottage beside a lake in the Laurentian mountains. When they returned to their house Dandy wrote to her mother, hoping her letter would be waiting at the Dyer house in Renwick when Anne and Morton returned from their trip around the world.

'And last week we did it,' she wrote. *'We actually signed a contract and we were declared husband and wife. It was really very easy and simple. Just Yvan and I and two witnesses. Now our relationship is legal. Yvan gave me a ring. It is platinum.'*

She stopped writing to look at her hand. The ring shone softly on her finger. She remembered how much she had disliked the engagement ring Jon had given her, how she had thought of it as a shackle, binding her to him. Now she was bound to Yvan, but she didn't mind because she was in love with him.

She chewed the end of her pen and looked out of the window of the living room. Sunlight slanted through the branches of the maple trees that lined the street and it made the red brick and white clapboard of the houses on the opposite side of the street gleam. Writing to her mother, trying to explain why she had run away with Yvan and had married him was proving to be much harder than she had thought. There was so much she wanted to tell Anne yet so much she couldn't tell her. Deciding what to put in and what to leave out was almost as difficult as making a programme for a computer, she thought ruefully.

'I wrote to Ted Wallis at D.B.M. resigning my position in the computer programming department before I left Renwick three weeks ago and have since received a letter from him accepting my resignation. I would like to go to work here, but will have to learn French first. Anyway Yvan says he doesn't want his wife to go to work and so far I'm enjoying being a woman of leisure. We belong to the yacht club on the lake here and I go there to play tennis most days. At the weekends we race Yvan's small yacht on the lake.'

She stopped writing again. How could she tell her mother how much she was in love with Yvan; how satisfying she found living with him. It was enough to admit to herself alone that although he and she had made love before they had married, the consummation of their marriage had been wonderful and romantic, more than it might have been if they had never made love, probably, because now that she was more knowledgeable about her own body as well as about Yvan's they were able to prolong the love play. No, she couldn't tell her mother anything like that. She couldn't tell anyone. It was something she would always keep to herself for the rest of her life.

'You're not to worry about me, Mother,' she wrote again quickly, fed up already with writing

the letter and wanting to finish it. *'I'm here because I want to be here and to be with Yvan. And I'm happier than I've ever been. I know it must seem strange to you and even Gramps (I'll be writing to him too) for me to get married to someone I met less than two months ago and so soon after I'd decided to marry Jon, but you see I fell in love with Yvan as soon as I met him.'*

The pen point hesitated and hovered over the paper. Dandy stared at the words she had just written *I fell in love. I am in love,* she whispered . . . *I'm in love with a wonderful guy.* She frowned and chewed the end of the pen again.

She was in love with Yvan more than ever, deeply and emotionally involved with him now, and everything was great while they were together. But when they were apart, when he was at work as he was this morning or when he went off himself without telling her where he had gone or why, doubts and suspicions would swell in her mind and she would realise that although she knew him physically she didn't know much more about his inner self than she had known before she had married him. He still kept that steel door closed against her invasion of his private thoughts and feelings and she was still reluctant to ask questions in case he snubbed her as he had that time on the hillside in Vermont in the snow.

If only she could have written to her mother that Yvan was in love with her the way she was in love with him. Oh, she knew he was physically attracted to her, but for how long would the state of sexual attraction last? What would happen when he grew tired of making love to her? And supposing he met another woman and became attracted to her?

I would run away. I wouldn't be able to bear it and I would run away, she vowed to herself.

She finished the letter, read it through, then pushed it into an envelope which she addressed and mailed on her way to the tennis courts. A week later Anne phoned her to say she had received the letter on her return to Renwick and they had a long conversation which ended with Anne inviting Dandy and Yvan to Renwick for the American Independence Day holiday at the beginning of July. Although surprised she seemed quite happy to accept Dandy's marriage to Yvan. *She's probably glad I'm out of her way at last,* thought Dandy.

The first weeks of June passed by in a golden blur with nothing happening to mar her happiness until one afternoon she returned home from playing tennis to find Yvan in the house.

'Why are you so early?' she exclaimed.

'Do you mind?' he asked teasingly, taking her in his arms and kissing her thoroughly.

'No, of course not? What's happened?'

'You'll remember me telling you about the company submitting a bid to build a dam in Colombia?' he said and when she nodded he continued. 'Well, it seems the Colombian power and light company that asked for the bids is interested in ours and would like to discuss it with those of us who were involved with the design. My boss, Pierre Chevrier, and I fly out to Bogota tomorrow. I have come home early to get ready and also to take you out to dinner.'

'How long are you going for?' Her voice came

out in a miserable croak. She felt devastated, as if all her blood were draining away; as if she were dying.

'A week, possibly longer. It depends on how the talks go.' He was obviously excited by the prospect and not thinking about leaving her behind.

'I'll come with you,' she said determinedly. 'I've always wanted to visit a South American country.'

In the process of taking clothes from the clothes closet in their bedroom to pack them in the suitcase he had put on the bed he turned to look at her, his face set in stern lines, his eyes cold.

'No. You will stay here. You can't come with me,' he said quietly but forcefully.

'Why not?' Rebelliousness began to stir in her.

'Because I don't want you to come. This is strictly a business trip and I won't have time to be with you much if you do come.'

'But that won't matter. I don't see much of you here but at least we meet every night and every weekend. It could be the same there.' She walked round to him and put her hand on his arm. 'Please, Yvan, let me come with you.'

'Not this time. It isn't possible,' he replied, shaking off her hand and beginning to fold a shirt.

Dandy stood as if frozen. It was the same as it had been in the cabin in Vermont the morning he had left and had told her she couldn't go with him; that she would be a complication he could do without. He didn't love her enough to want her with him.

'But what will I do while you're away?' she whispered. 'Oh, what will I do?'

'What you have been doing these past few weeks,' he said turning to smile at her and putting his hands on her shoulders and drawing her towards him. 'Playing tennis, looking after this house for me, taking the boat out on the lake. There is plenty for you to do and before you realise it I'll be back.'

'But ... but how will I know. ...' She paused, realising that what she was about to say would probably infuriate him.

'How will you know what?' he asked, putting his arms about her and holding her closely.

'How will I know you'll be ... be faithful to me while you're away?' she whispered, her voice muffled as she spoke into the stuff of his suit jacket. At once he stiffened and his hands hard on her arms he pushed her away from him. His eyes blazed with blue fire.

'You will just have to trust me,' he said, taut-lipped. 'As I will trust you to be faithful to me. That is what marriage is all about. Or didn't you know?'

'Yes, I know. I ... I just wondered if you did,' she murmured and flung herself against him suddenly, her arms going around him, holding him to her desperately. 'Oh, Yvan, please don't go. Let them send someone else. It's cruel of them, your company I mean, to send you away when we've been married only a few weeks.'

'I asked if I could go,' he said pushing her from him again, 'I want to go. I want the company to get that contract and I want to be the one who supervises the construction of the dam. It is what I like doing most. Please understand. It is my work, my career and it's important to me.'

'More important than I am?' she challenged him.

'Not more, but equally as important.' He gave her an exasperated glance. 'I didn't think you would behave so childishly. I thought you would understand why I have to go.'

'Oh, I understand why you have to go,' she retorted, cut to the quick by his taunt about her behaviour being childish. 'I just can't understand why I have to stay behind here, why I can't go with you and most of all why you don't want me with you.'

She saw the steel door close down at the back of his eyes. Turning away from her he continued to pack without saying another word and she knew she had lost the argument in the way she always lost to him. She had no way of breaking through that impassive silence he could maintain; no way of bending his inflexible will.

'I may not be here when you come back,' she said, using her only weapon. 'I might go away too.'

'To see your mother, perhaps?' he said calmly, not in the least perturbed. 'That is a good idea. If you do go be sure to leave a note for me saying where you've gone.'

It wasn't the answer she had hoped for. She had hoped he might react passionately. She had hoped he might have played the jealous, possessive husband and insist she be there in their home when he returned. Either that, or that he might have relented and let her go with him.

All that evening while they dined at a nearby exclusive restaurant and later when he made love to her in their bed she hoped he would relent. She was so afraid of what might happen while he was away from her, that the spell of happiness in which she had been living since he had brought her to Montreal might be broken in some way.

But when morning came he hadn't changed his mind and he left to fly to Colombia without her.

CHAPTER SEVEN

A WEEK after Yvan's departure for Colombia Dandy returned to the town house late one afternoon, having been shopping in Montreal. Only the day before she had heard from Yvan, a telex message sent out to her from the company offices telling her that he would not be home for another week. As a result of receiving the message she had decided to drive down to Renwick the next day to visit Anne and Morton and to stay with them over the July 4th holiday, as she had been invited. If Yvan came back while she was away he could either drive down to join her at the Dyer house or he could wait until she returned to Montreal.

She was in the kitchen drinking iced tea, because the day was very hot, and wondering what to eat for her evening meal when the front door bell rang. Thinking it was one of her tennis friends come to ask her to play a game that evening, she went to the front door and opened it.

A strange woman was standing on the doorstep. She was tall and was beautifully dressed in a suit of black silk and a crisp white blouse with ruffles at the neck. A wide hat of black felt was tilted rakishly on her sleek upswept blonde hair. She stared at Dandy with surprise.

'*Excusez moi,*' she said. 'I think that maybe I make a mistake. I look for the house of Monsieur Yvan Rambert. I was told that he live at number four hundred and two, but perhaps I get the number wrong.'

'No, you haven't got it wrong. He does live here, but he isn't home right now,' said Dandy. 'Perhaps I could give him a message for you when he does come home.'

'You clean the house for him?' queried the woman, her glance flickering disdainfully over Dandy's jeans and cotton blouse.

'Oh no ... I mean, yes I do ... but I'm not a cleaning woman,' replied Dandy hurriedly. 'I'm Dandy Rambert. I'm his wife.'

The woman's sea-green eyes opened very wide and her finely plucked eyebrows arched incredulously.

'Yvan is married to you?' she exclaimed and shook her head from side to side. 'I do not believe it. You are kidding me.'

'No, I'm not. We were married last month. Look.' Dandy held out her left hand and the wide platinum band on her third finger glinted in the sunlight. The woman stared at it for a moment and then looked up.

'But you are an American,' she said slowly.

'Anything wrong in that?' retorted Dandy, belligerently.

'No, not really. It is just that I would not have expected Yvan to have married someone so young.' The woman touched a hand to her temple and closed her eyes. *'Excusez-moi,'* she whispered. 'I do not feel well, I have been under great stress recently and now, hearing about Yvan's marriage to you has come as something of a shock. I am a very old friend of his. He may have told you about me. My name is Nicole ... Nicole Bujold. Would you mind if I came in and sat down for a few minutes . . . perhaps a drink of water.'

'Of course,' said Dandy quickly and generously. The woman did look very pale. 'Please come in. Come right through to the living room and sit down. I'll get you a drink. Are you sure water is enough? I could make tea or coffee for you.'

'Water,' whispered the woman and sank gracefully on to the pale grey contemporary-styled sofa.

Alarmed by the woman's behaviour Dandy rushed into the kitchen and filled a glass with cold water then hurried back to the living room. Nicole Bujold was looking better, not so pale, and was lighting a cigarette.

'Thank you,' she said with a charming smile as she took the glass of water from Dandy. 'I apologise. I'm not normally given to feeling faint.'

'Did you say your name is Nicole?' asked Dandy as she sat down. 'I haven't heard that name before,' she said. Her brain was clicking fast as it absorbed and computed the information it had been given. This woman must be Niki, the woman of Yvan's dreams.

'It isn't unusual in France and I come from Paris,' Nicole smiled again, a small smile of reminiscence as she leaned forward and put the glass of water on the coffee table. 'Yvan and I met there, years ago. As I have said we are very good friends, very close.'

'Is this your first time in Montreal?' asked Dandy politely.

'Oh, no. I have been here many times to visit Yvan. For the past two years I have been living in Ottawa with my husband Jules. He represented a

French government department as a trade commissioner.' Nicole sighed sadly. 'Unfortunately he died suddenly, a few weeks ago. A massive brain haemorrhage, so shocking.' She looked for and found a small white handkerchief and dabbed at her eyes with it.

'I'm sorry,' murmured Dandy inadequately.

'I'm still suffering a little from the shock, you understand,' said Nicole plaintively.

'Does Yvan know that your husband has died?' Dandy asked.

'I do not know. I can only think that he does not because if he had known I am sure he would have. . . .' Nicole's voice shook slightly and glanced appealingly at Dandy. 'Forgive me for saying this but Yvan and I have always been so close that if he had known Jules had died I'm sure he would have come to see me to offer me comfort.' She paused, then added without looking at Dandy, 'I'm sure he wouldn't have married you.' She looked sideways at Dandy. 'Is it possible that Yvan hasn't told you anything about me, about his . . . his friendship with me?'

'No, he never has,' replied Dandy frankly, wishing fervently that he had, wishing too that she had persisted in questioning him about Niki, the woman he had professed to love when he had been dreaming at the cabin in Vermont.

'He did not tell me about you either,' said Nicole with a sigh. She gave Dandy another underbrowed glance. 'I hope he hasn't deceived you.'

I hope he hasn't, too, thought Dandy, feeling a chill run through her.

'In what way would he do that?' she queried.

'You seem very friendly and open. It would be easy for a sophisticated man like Yvan to take advantage of you. I suspect you haven't known him for very long. When did you meet him?'

'In . . . in March,' admitted Dandy, unable to lie.

'I see.' Nicole nodded. 'Last time I was with Yvan he said something about having to get married or he would be cut out of his father's will.' She paused and looked enquiringly at Dandy. 'Have you met any of Yvan's family yet?' she asked.

'No, but I'm hoping to meet General Rambert and Yvan's sister in the summer. They are coming to stay with us in July. General Rambert had written to Yvan saying he wanted to see him soon. Apparently he has been ill and. . . .'

'Yes, that is what Yvan told me.' Nicole interrupted her. 'And he also said the old man wanted him to be married before he made his will leaving his considerable fortune to Yvan. He had threatened, it seems, to leave everything, his estate in Normandy and all his investments, to charity if Yvan didn't marry and have a family to carry on the name. Yvan said nothing of this to you, about the pressure being put on him?'

'No, he told me nothing of that,' said Dandy weakly. *And I asked no questions because I didn't want to be snubbed,* she remembered miserably.

'Of course he wouldn't,' murmured Nicole, nodding her head. 'He is very clever, that Yvan, very subtle. He deceives you, making you think he is in love with you, I've no doubt, so that you will agree to marry him and at the same time he deceives his father. I suppose he hasn't told you either why he left France and came to Canada?'

'I know that he quarrelled with his father,' muttered Dandy.

'That is so, but do you know what they quarrelled about?' asked Nicole, leaning forward.

'Not really.'

'It was about Yvan's relationship with me. You see unfortunately, I didn't meet Yvan until after I had married Jules. I fell in love with him. It was easy, believe me, for he was young and handsome and Jules, although rich, was twenty years older than I.' Nicole shrugged. 'I would have liked to have divorced Jules to marry Yvan, but Jules would not hear of it. So Yvan and I became lovers. The General eventually found out about our affair and was furious. Since Yvan is his only son he wanted him to marry a nice young woman he had chosen for him. Yvan refused to marry her, they quarrelled and Yvan left France. For a while, I did not see him, but when Jules was posted to Ottawa, we were able to renew our relationship.' Nicole sighed and looked down at the handkerchief which she was twisting between her fingers. 'If only he could have waited a few more weeks, we could have been married at last. He could have married me instead of you. You see he loves me and always has and if he had waited just a little longer . . . oh, why didn't he wait? Why didn't he wait?'

Overcome by her distress Nicole dabbed again at her eyes with the handkerchief.

'You'll have to ask Yvan that,' said Dandy in a cold little voice. 'When he comes back from Colombia. He won't be back for another week.

Why don't you come to see him then and ask him why he didn't wait?'

'You wouldn't object if I came to see him?' Nicole looked up in surprise.

'Not at all,' said Dandy rising to her feet, wanting the other woman to go, 'You see I won't be here. I'm going to visit my mother for a while. And now would you please excuse me? I have a date to play tennis this evening and I'd like to change my clothes.' The last was a lie, but it gave no option to the French woman.

'But of course. I will leave at once.' Nicole rose to her feet too. 'You have been very kind. I feel much better now. I have to drive back to Ottawa this evening so I had best be on my way.' At the front door she turned and smiled, '*À bientôt*, Dandy. I'm pleased to have met you and I'm sure now that you know about Yvan and me you will do what you think best for all concerned. Goodbye.'

'Goodbye.' Dandy watched Nicole walk down the path and get into the expensive black car that was parked at the curbside in front of the house. Then she closed the door quietly and stood in the hallway for a few moments trying to control the anger that was surging up in her.

She was angry mostly with herself for having been so naïve and trusting; for not having asked Yvan about Nicole, or Niki as he called her; and for not having taken enough notice of her grandfather's warning: *Yvan is in love with Nicole*.

It had happened after all. The spell of happiness in which she had been living had been broken. Yvan had deceived her and had stampeded her into marrying him so that his marriage would be a *fait accompli* when his father came to visit him; so that he wouldn't be cut out of his father's will. Knowing her to be in love with him and so easily deceived, he had married her, but only because he hadn't been able to marry Nicole.

What would he say when he knew that Nicole was free to marry him at last, now that Jules Bujold had died? What would he do? Ask her for a divorce so soon after marrying her? Or would he continue his affair with Nicole, hoping she wouldn't guess he had a mistress?

Oh, no. She wasn't going to have that. She hadn't married Jon because she had found out he had been two-timing her. So what was she going to do? Whatever was best for all concerned, Nicole had suggested. But what could that be?

Right now she couldn't do anything because Yvan wasn't there. Oh, how she wished that he was. How she wished he was coming home that evening and that she could tell him that his friend . . . his very *close* friend . . . Nicole had been to see him. She found she was clenching her hands and grinding her teeth as jealousy swept through her. A woman called Nicole had stepped into her life unexpectedly and had poisoned her mind, making her suspicious of Yvan and spoiling her delicate, vulnerable relationship with him. No, not her relationship, how she hated that word and its modern connotations, spoiling her *marriage* to him.

She couldn't stay in this house any longer. She would have to leave. Yes, that was what she would do. She would leave now and drive south. It wouldn't take her long to pack, and be on her way to Renwick. Or should she go to the cabin in Vermont? No, Renwick would be better. She was expected there and Yvan had never been in the Dyer House, so there would be no memories of him there to haunt her.

Within three quarters of an hour she was ready to leave and sitting at Yvan's desk in the small 'den', writing the note he had asked her to leave for him if she should go away. While she had been packing she had decided what to do. Without Yvan she might as well not be in Montreal and when he learned that Nicole was free he would regret having married herself in such a hurry. So she would do what she thought best for all concerned and most of all best for Yvan, whom she loved. She would leave him and put an end to their brief marriage so that he could marry the woman he loved. That was best.

So she wrote quickly, before she could change her mind:

'I have decided it was a mistake for us to marry so I am ending the marriage now by returning this ring to you. I know about you and Nicole. I have always known, ever since Vermont, but I thought it was all over. Being the way I am I can't stay married to you knowing that if you could have waited you could have married her. It is best this way. Love, Dandy.'

She read through what she had written and then added on impulse something she had once said to him: *Oh Yvan, how could you? How could you?* Then she slipped off her wedding ring and put it in an envelope with the note. She addressed the envelope with his name and left it on the desk.

An hour later she was on the wide road going south towards the border with the sun sliding down the sky on her right. It was just after midnight when she arrived at the Dyer house, where Anne had stayed up to welcome her, having been warned by a phone call that Dandy was on her way.

Pleased to see Anne Dandy hugged her and kissed her.

'Mm, you smell nice,' she said with a little laugh. 'Just like my mother.'

'I'm glad you approve,' said Anne lightly. 'But why have you come without Yvan? Will he be coming at the weekend?'

'I don't know. He ... he's in Colombia right now on business.' Dandy's voice shook a little but she refused to let the tears well in her eyes. 'Oh, Mom I've really done it this time. I've really got into an awful mess.'

'Then you'd best sit down and tell me about it,' said Anne patiently.

'I can't tell you all of it now,' replied Dandy. 'I can only tell you that I've realised I shouldn't have married him. You see he doesn't love me. He loves another woman and I only found out today ... that she's still around and that if he hadn't married me, if he'd waited a little longer he could have married her because her husband has died. Oh, it's just the same as if I'd married Jon and he'd continued to see Jenny and I can't take it ... so ... so. ...'

'You've run away again,' supplied Anne dryly. 'That figures.' She sighed. 'Oh, Dandy, when are you going to grow up?' She gave Dandy a slightly mocking glance. 'I suppose you're hoping he'll follow you when he returns to Montreal and finds you've left.'

'I suppose I am,' muttered Dandy. 'But I'm not expecting him to when he finds out that . . . that Nicole's husband died and that she's free at last to marry him. He loves her, you see, and always has.'

'Then why did you marry him?'

'Because he asked me to and because I love him. Oh, what a fool I've been, what a fool. Why do I make so many mistakes? Why?'

'Because it's the only way you can learn, I guess,' replied Anne.

'What did Gramps say about me marrying Yvan?' Dandy asked curiously.

'Not much. He was surprised and just a little concerned about you, but he wouldn't say why. I guess he likes Yvan but he didn't really approve of the way you married in a hurry. He thought you should have waited until Morton and I returned. Morton felt the same.'

'He would,' said Dandy fiercely, then added contritely, 'I'm sorry. I am beginning to realise Morton does what he does for the best and I suppose I should be grateful to him for trying to be a father to me.'

That night she slept in the bedroom that had always been hers when she had lived in that house. She slept heavily and when she awoke the next day she felt dull and lethargic and while she was eating breakfast she experienced a desire to be sick to her stomach. She said nothing of the feeling of nausea to her mother and spent the day visiting D.B.M. and talking with her boss in the department of computer programming and other friends she met there. Nothing seemed to have changed in the department and they hadn't even found someone to replace her.

'We'd have you back any time,' said Ted Wallis, head of the department. 'How about commuting between here and Montreal?'

Later the same day she met Sallyanne and they went to a restaurant for dinner together.

'Jon has gone to New York, to work for a Public Relations company there,' Sallyanne informed her. 'His parents are mad, of course, that he left D.B.M.'

'And Jenny?' asked Dandy.

'She's gone too. They're living together.'

By the end of the week Dandy was really becoming worried about the way she felt and eventually, at the suggestion of her mother, she made an appointment to see the family doctor. He listened to her description of the vague changes she had been aware of in herself during the past month and then gave her some tests.

'Sounds to me as if you're pregnant,' he said, 'but the tests will confirm it.'

'When will you have the results?'

'Give me a call tomorrow morning,' he replied.

In a daze she left his offices and drove back across the river. The weather was perfect, a clear blue sky arching above the sun shining down relentlessly so that the inside of the car was baking hot and she had to open all the vents and let down a window. When she reached the other side of the river, instead of driving straight to the house she turned down a lane to an old wharf jutting out into the glittering blue-grey water of the wide Hudson. Two boys were sitting on the wharf fishing and on the other side of the river the Catskills were patterned in varying greens.

A baby. Hers and Yvan's baby, conceived, she

guessed now, in the cabin in Vermont that first time they had made love together, when she had been too overwhelmed by desire to bother with any precautions. *A baby.* What was she going to do with it? She was going to keep it of course. She couldn't do otherwise, because the child would be a product of her love for Yvan. She supposed she would have to tell Yvan as soon as he came to Renwick. *If* he came to Renwick.

Today was the last day of June. He should be back in Montreal by now, if all had gone well in Colombia. He should have found her note by now. But he hadn't called the Dyer House to find out if she was there yet and it was possible he wouldn't come.

And if he did come she wouldn't tell him she was pregnant. Pride forbade that course of action. He would think she had told him so he would feel responsible and would be honour bound to stay married to her. No, she wouldn't tell him. She wouldn't tell anyone, yet. She would hug this secret to herself as long as she could.

Next day when she called the doctor's office she was informed that the tests had confirmed she was pregnant and the knowledge immediately affected her way of life. She took more care and interest in what she ate, cutting out smoking and drinking, not that she had ever indulged in either very much. She had someone else to care for, someone who wasn't alive and kicking yet, it was true, but who would be soon.

June gave way to July and preparations for the Independence day holiday. There was no call from Yvan to say he was coming to join her at Renwick and she assumed that he had decided to spend the time with Nicole, who had probably been to see him by now. July 4th dawned and as always the whole of Renwick turned out to line the main street and watch the parade of local bands and organisations go by. As usual Dandy stood at the same corner where she had stood with Anne and Morton over the years to watch, too. A few times, in the past, she had marched in the parade; once when she had been a member of the Girl Scouts of America and later when she had played the clarinet in the High School Band. This time she was there to watch and applaud Sallyanne who was a majorette for the High School Alumni band.

When the parade was over Dandy went back to the Dyer House with Morton and Anne, ate a lunch of cold meats and salad and then lay down for a while in her room. At three o'clock she got up, changed into a white linen skirt and a bright pink cotton V-necked top and went downstairs.

Every July 4th, ever since she could remember, Anne and Morton had held a party, drinks on the sun-deck and in the garden followed by a serve-yourself dinner of hamburgers, hot dogs, and various salads, followed by strawberry shortcake and coffee. Afterwards there was always a firework display in the garden. This day, for the first time in years, Dandy had agreed to help Anne serve drinks and dinner. Usually, since she had entered her teens, she had gone off with her friends to attend more boisterous parties.

But now she was responsible for someone else, for the unborn baby and she no longer felt a feverish desire to party with her friends. Maybe she had really grown up at last, she thought with a wry grin.

The people who came to the Dyer's party were always the same, a group of friends and relatives who had known each other for years. Morton's two sisters were there with their husbands. Both of them greeted Dandy coolly, they had never hidden their disapproval of her. One of Morton's nieces was there too, up from Virginia to visit her parents with her husband and to show off the fact that she, too, was pregnant and, as she watched her cousin-by-marriage holding court as various relatives and friends gathered around her to offer congratulations, Dandy was suddenly tempted to bang on a table and announce that she was also pregnant and qualified for congratulations.

But she didn't. She couldn't embarrass Anne and Morton by doing it. Oh, yes, she had really grown up. Never again would she embarrass them by openly defiant behaviour.

She was in the kitchen helping Marcie to set food out on the long table so that everyone could help themselves when she heard the deep voice of her grandfather in the family room behind her. She stopped what she was doing and went through into the other room.

'Gramps, it's good to see you.' She flung herself into his held out arms and hugged him. 'We thought you weren't coming.'

'Well, I was a mite delayed. You see I had to go up to Montreal yesterday,' he replied. 'We drove as far as the cabin yesterday evening and came on here this afternoon, didn't we?' He turned to the man who was standing behind him.

Dandy stared incredulously at the man with wide flat shoulders and lean hips whose aquiline features looked as if they had been chiselled from cream-coloured marble and whose blue-grey eyes gleamed with vivid light, startling between their black lashes.

'Now don't go staring at him as if you'd never seen him before,' Douglas chided her cheerfully. 'Get him something to drink, show him around and introduce him to a few people. Remember he's a stranger here.'

'Douglas, at last. I was beginning to get anxious, thinking you weren't coming to the party,' Anne appeared, walking in through the wide patio doorway from the sun-deck. 'What took you so long?' She noticed Yvan and her eyes widened, 'I don't think we've met before,' she said softly, suddenly going all feminine, her eyelashes fluttering and a pretty pink colour rising in her cheeks.

'This is Yvan Rambert,' said Douglas chuckling. 'I guess you've heard about him from Dandy,' he added, winking at his granddaughter. 'Yvan has come to celebrate Independence Day with us. You know the French. Like us they're all for liberty, equality and fraternity. Yvan, meet your mother-in-law, Anne Dyer.'

'Je suis enchanté, madame,' murmured Yvan, smiling. He was at his most charming, taking Anne's proffered hand in his and raising it to his lips, making up to her blatantly, as if he couldn't help flirting with a pretty woman even if she was about twelve years older than he was, thought Dandy acidly. He had never looked at her like that and he had never flirted with her.

Turning on her heel she went back to the kitchen. Her heart was hammering against her ribs, her cheeks were burning and her head felt several sizes larger than usual. Yvan had come and she should be dancing and singing, letting him and the whole world know that she was glad he was there. But all she felt was this terrible confusion; love and hate, desire and jealousy; jealousy of her own mother because Yvan has smiled and had spoken to Anne but had only stared coldly and severely at herself, the woman he was married to.

'Dandy, you can come out of your daydreams and tell the folks they can come along in and help themselves,' Marcia spoke sharply and bossily. 'I guess everything is out now. Tell the folks to go round the table this way and take a plate from that pile. Okay?'

'Okay,' muttered Dandy and left the kitchen by the back door to walk round to the garden and up to the sun-deck to tell everyone to go in and help themselves to food. Nothing was going to make her go through the family room again. *Nothing*. If Yvan wanted to talk to her he would have to make the first move, and then wait until she was good and ready to talk to him. Pride, native and stubborn, forbade that she behave any differently.

Most of the guests had been through the kitchen and had helped themselves, some of them staying to talk to Dandy, and they were scattered about in the dining room and in the living room eating and talking when Douglas came into the kitchen followed by Anne and Yvan.

'Mom, I think I'd like to quit now,' Dandy said in a low voice to Anne, keeping her back turned to Yvan. 'I guess the aunts will help you and Marcie with the clearing up.' She glanced at her watch. It was almost eight o'clock. 'I promised Sallyanne and some other friends I'd join them at her apartment to watch the firework display in the town park.'

'But we'll be having our own firework display,'
Anne protested and as Dandy made for the back
door she followed her and added in a whisper.
'You can't leave right now. Yvan has come to see
you.'

'Then he'll just have to come with me to
Sallyanne's won't he?' retorted Dandy and
opening the door stepped outside.

Down the driveway to the road she walked.
Behind the Catskills the sun was going down,
streaking the greenish-blue sky with bars of
crimson and orange light. Already dusk was falling
like a purple veil about the houses which edged the
river road, and lights glimmered yellow through
the foliage of the trees. The warm air was full of
the scents of summer flowers and every so often a
firework would explode and a shower of red, white
and blue sparks would hang in the sky like a
blossom. From gardens where other parties were
going on music and voices floated out.

She had lied to Anne about going to Sallyanne's.
She had no intention of going to watch the
firework display in the park. She had hoped to
stay and watch Morton's firework display. She
hadn't watched it for a long time and his display
was always an artistic creation. He thought about
it and planned it for weeks ahead of time,
choosing the fireworks carefully from a catalogue
sent to him from a fireworks outlet in North
Carolina.

She reached the place where the river road
ended and where Devlin road went up the hill
right to Main Street and the narrow lane went left,
downhill to the old wharf. Behind her she could
hear footsteps, crisp and somehow determined on

the surface of the river road. Turning into the lane, already dark, she walked down to the wharf.

The river glimmered with reflected light from the setting sun except where purple shadows lurked under pilings that supported the wharf. On the opposite shore the mountains were black cut-out shapes against a band of orange sky. Dandy walked to the edge of the wharf and looked down into the water. *Whoosh. Pop, pop, pop.* A rocket firework shot up into the air above the river and burst, raining down a shower of sparks.

'Dandy.' Yvan spoke behind her but she didn't turn. 'Why did you walk out of the house like that without saying anything to me?' he demanded. 'I came here especially to be with you and all you have done is avoid me.'

'Well, you didn't seem to want to say anything to me,' she retorted, still not turning. 'You were far more interested in my mother than in me. Anyway, why have you come?'

It cost her a lot to keep her voice cool and her shoulders straight.

He stepped to her side, took hold of her elbow and swung her around to face him. In the last of the light she could see his eyes, gleaming coldly like the tips of daggers. He put a hand in the side pocket of his light grey linen sports jacket and took a piece of paper out of it.

'I've come for an explanation of this,' he replied tautly and thrust the paper at her. She looked at it knowing it was the note she had left for him on the desk in the study of their house in Montreal.

CHAPTER EIGHT

'YOU could have written to me and asked for an explanation. You didn't have to come and see me,' she said, still cool, but looking at him, looking at the paper instead. 'I thought it was quite clear, what I'd put in it.'

He muttered something in French that sounded as if it would be rude and his breath hissed savagely as he drew it in. His hand tightened on her arm and she tensed, sensing that his control over his anger was near to breaking point. She forced herself to stay still, but she was quiveringly aware in every nerve of his physical presence, of the throbbing hardness of his body, sheathed as it was in fine linen and cotton and it seemed to her that all the juices in her body rushed together to one part. She felt suddenly swollen with the longing to lean against him and to touch him, to caress his face, ruffle his hair, kiss his lips and invite him to touch her.

'You would try the patience of a saint,' he growled between his teeth. 'And I have never pretended to be one of them. Where should I have written? In this,' he shook the paper under her nose, 'you didn't tell me where you'd gone.'

'But I thought you would guess I'd come here. Before you went to Colombia you said that if I decided to come and see my mother I was to leave a note. . . .'

'Telling me where you'd gone,' he interrupted

162

her roughly. 'This doesn't. This only tells me you've decided for some reason that you want to end our marriage because you've found out about Nicole. How did you find out about her?'

'She ... she came to see you while you were away. She was very upset when she learned that I was your wife. She told me all about your affair with her and how her husband had died and how she wished you had waited a while longer before marrying me.' She paused for breath and pulled her arm free of his hand. 'I decided I wasn't going to put up with it,' she continued glaring at him. 'I hate men who two-time their wives. I loathe deception of that sort. I found out that Nicole is your lover and has been for years and so I left you. If you and she want to marry now that her husband has died you can go ahead and divorce me.'

He was silent for a few moments and she couldn't make out the expression on his face now that the light was fading fast, but she could hear him breathing hard as if he was having a struggle to control himself. At last he spoke.

'You believed her,' he accused, his voice silky soft with menace. 'You had so little trust in me that you believed everything a woman you'd never met in your life before told you.'

'Well, it wasn't hard to believe her,' she retorted. 'I knew all about you being lovers and I know you're in love with her because I'd heard you say so.'

'When? When did you ever hear me say I love Nicole?' he demanded harshly, anger breaking through his control at last so that he reached out, grasped her by the arms and shook her.

'The first time we ever slept together at the cabin in Vermont,' she retorted, tossing back her head and looking up at him. 'And now let go of me. You're hurting me.'

'Am I?' he replied sardonically but he let go of her arms and thrust his hands into his pants pockets. Fireworks blazed in the sky behind him and she guessed they had been sent up from the garden of the Dyer house. 'But then perhaps you deserve to be hurt, somehow,' he continued his voice soft again, 'for the pain you've inflicted on me by your irresponsible behaviour in leaving that note for me to find, and for going away without telling me where you were going.'

'I thought you would know where I'd gone,' she said again defensively. 'And I thought you'd understand the note.'

There was silence. More fireworks popped. Dandy turned away and looked out at the river and across at the dark blur of the mountains. Lights twinkled among the trees on the opposite shore and some were reflected in the water.

'I did it for the best,' she muttered. 'At least I thought I was doing what was best at the time.' She turned back to him, trying again to see his face and failing because it was quite dark, down there on the old wharf. 'I know you love Nicole and that you would have married her instead of me if you'd known that her husband had died. I know you love her because I'd heard you say you did when you were dreaming about her the night we slept together in Vermont. . . .'

'What?' His exclamation was sharp, like a pistol shot. 'You heard me say what when I was dreaming? Tell me exactly what I said.'

'I didn't understand all of what you said because you spoke in French, but I did recognise some of it. You said. . . .' Her voice faltered and fell to a whisper, 'Oh, you said quite clearly "Niki, *je t'aime, je t'aime beaucoup*" and then you began to caress me so I woke you up. Don't you remember?'

Again he drew in his breath sharply and was silent for a while, peering down at her, as if he too was trying to see the expression on her face.

'All I remember is waking up and finding you beside me in the bed,' he said eventually. '*Mon Dieu*, my subconscious was really working overtime that night, wasn't it?' he added with a dreary laugh. 'I'm not surprised you woke me up.' He was silent for a few more seconds, then said slowly. 'But I wasn't talking to Nicole. I wasn't dreaming about her. I was dreaming about another woman.'

'Oh, don't lie to me,' Dandy cried out. 'Please don't lie to me. I won't be able to bear it if you lie.'

'I'm not lying.' He almost spat the words at her.

'Yes, you are. I know you were talking to Nicole and calling her by your pet name for her. I know too that you continued your affair with her when she came to Ottawa with her husband because she told me herself she used to go to Montreal to see you. And she was with you when you first met Gramps. He told me she was. He told me you had a beautiful woman with you called Niki and that she was also from France and that there was something pretty powerful going on between you and her and. . . .'

'That woman was not Nicole Bujold,' he shouted at her, just as a giant firework burst over

the river, lighting up everything. He muttered
some imprecation in French and she saw him
rake a hand through his hair before the light
faded. 'My God, it's difficult to stop you when
you have made up your mind about something,'
he growled. 'You've got everything wrong. And
if anyone has been lying it is Nicole. She always
was a liar.'

'You deny then that you used to know her when
you lived in Paris and that you had an affair with
her?' she demanded accusingly.

'No, I don't deny that. I can't. That part is true.
But the affair didn't last long and it didn't
continue when she came Canada. Oh, she tried to
re-kindle it several times, always phoning me and
even coming to my apartment before I bought the
house.' She made a little sound of distress and he
paused for a moment. Then he said, 'Don't you
believe me?'

'I'm finding it very hard to believe that there are
two women, one called Nicole and one called
Niki,' she said, her voice half-choked. 'It seems to
be too much of a coincidence to be true and I
don't want to hear any more of your lies.'

Whirling, she ran towards the lane, hearing him
call after her. Up the lane she ran to the river road
and along it to the Dyer House. Everyone was out
in the garden watching the fireworks display.
Unnoticed Dandy made her way upstairs to her
bedroom and entered it. She shut the door behind
her and turned the key in the lock.

For a long time she sat alone in the darkness,
watching the fireworks through the window, trying
to calm herself and going over and over in her
mind everything that Yvan had said to her; trying

to convince herself that Niki wasn't Nicole and vice-versa, that Nicole wasn't Niki.

After a while the fireworks stopped. She could hear people saying goodnight and cars starting up. Everything became quiet. She switched on the bedside lamp and looked at her watch. It was almost eleven o'clock and Yvan hadn't come looking for her. But then how could he look for her when he didn't know where to look? Maybe he had left. Maybe he had been so angry when she had accused him of lying he had gone away and she would never see him again.

She undressed and put on her nightgown, visited the bathroom and returned to the bedroom to brush her hair. Twenty minutes went by and nothing happened. Yvan didn't come so, after pulling on a dressing-gown, she left the room and went downstairs.

Hearing Anne's voice coming from the living room she tip-toed to the entrance and peeped into the room. Anne was sitting on the sofa, her red-gold hair glinting in the electric light. Sitting opposite to her and listening intently was Yvan.

'Oh, so this is where you both are,' said Dandy airily and they turned to look at her.

'I didn't know you'd come back. We've been waiting for you,' said Anne rising to her feet. Polite as ever Yvan stood up too. His face was set in hard lines and Dandy thought he looked daggers at her again.

'I've been back for some time,' she said, shrugging her shoulders. 'Am I interrupting something?' She looked from Yvan to her mother and back to him, feeling jealousy twisting within her.

'No. Yvan and I were just having a little talk, getting to know each other while we waited for you,' replied Anne serenely. She turned back to Yvan. 'Now I won't have to show you to your bedroom. Dandy will show you. Goodnight, Yvan.'

'Goodnight, Anne,' Yvan replied quietly. 'And thank you.'

'It was my pleasure,' said Anne, giving him her warmest smile. 'Goodnight, love,' she said affectionately to Dandy as she passed her. 'See you in the morning.'

Anne left the room. Dandy advanced slowly into it and sat down on an arm of the sofa. Yvan stayed standing.

'Did you go to the firework display in the park?' he asked coolly.

'No. I . . . I came back here.'

'Then where have you been all this time?' he asked, stepping over to her and frowning at her in puzzlement.

'In my bedroom.'

'All the time? But why?'

'I wanted to think about what you'd said. I . . . I thought you might have come looking for me but it . . . it seems you preferred to talk to my mother. I know she's very pretty and she knows how to talk to men. . . .'

'Stop it, Dandy,' he cautioned her softly. 'Stop guessing. Stop imagining something that isn't there. You're usually wrong when you do it, just as you were wrong to believe everything Nicole Bujold told you and to accuse me of lying to you.'

'Oh, I want to believe you, I want to,' she muttered piteously gazing up at him, 'You've no idea how I want to believe you and not Nicole, but it's difficult.'

'Why don't you ask your grandfather to describe Niki to you if you still don't believe Nicole is not Niki?' he asked. The shadow she had seen before passed across his face, a darkening caused by some deeply felt emotion. He rubbed his fingers across his eyes and then turned away from her, presenting his back to her as if he didn't want her to see his face. 'If you ask Doug what Niki looked like you'll find that she wasn't at all like Nicole,' he said.

'What was she like?' asked Dandy, feeling she was on the verge of a discovery she didn't want to make and forcing herself to face up to a truth which she sensed was going to hurt her far more than anything Nicole Bujold had told her. 'Yvan, please tell me,' she pleaded.

He turned to look at her. His face was very pale.

'She was dark-haired and brown-eyed, like you in colouring but she was smaller. *Petite*,' he replied in a strained voice. 'Her name was Anik but I called her Niki. We were going to be married last January, soon after New Year's Day, but she was killed.'

Dandy sat still, feeling a chill in her veins. Memories of the two days she had spent with him at the cabin in Vermont flickered through her mind like a silent movie; memories of the questions she had asked which he hadn't answered; memories of the way he had kept her at a distance all the time. Now she understood why he had seemed so withdrawn and reserved. Now she knew why the woman he loved had not been with him.

'You should have told me,' she said softly. 'If you had told me about Anik I wouldn't have believed that Nicole was the woman you loved and I wouldn't have believed her when she told me you are still lovers, or that you would have married her instead of me if you'd known her husband had died.'

She was shocked by the look on his face. He looked as if he had been to hell and back. Talking about Anik had done that to him. He had loved the woman, really and truly, and had lost her.

'Why didn't you tell me about Anik?' she persisted, her voice shaking a little with the intensity of the emotions that were sweeping through her; empathy for him in his bereavement and regret because she had been too hasty in judging him, too quick to believe what Nicole had said.

'I couldn't . . . and talking about it now is like being split apart and having my insides dragged out, like being drawn and quartered,' he confessed bitterly.

'But it must be done.' She sprang to her feet and went to him. She put a hand on his arm, her fingers pressing through the linen of the jacket sleeve to the flesh and bone beneath as she tried to convey her feelings to him. 'Tell me how she was killed,' she urged.

'It was a car accident. A drunk driver hit her. His car crossed the median of the highway, out of control and crashed into her car, head-on. She was on her way to meet me. Her car was small and it was crushed. Like that.' He hit the palms of his hands together and held them pressed together so that there was no space between them. 'So was she.' His voice was hard. 'There was nothing left.'

'Oh, no.' The cry was torn from Dandy and she flung her arms around him to hold him closely, trying to ease a little of the pain that telling her must have caused him to feel. 'I'm sorry, so sorry.'

'Don't say that. I don't want your pity,' he said harshly. 'That's why I didn't tell you at the cabin in Vermont or afterwards. I don't want your pity.' He pushed her away from him. 'And I wouldn't have told you now if you hadn't run away and left that stupid little note for me to find.' He looked down at her coldly. 'And if you hadn't called me a liar,' he added. 'So now that you know about Niki, do you believe that Nicole is not my lover any more? That affair with her happened a year ago and caused me nothing but trouble,' he made a repudiating gesture. 'I never want to have anything to do with her again and I have told her that many times.'

'What sort of trouble? Please tell me. Can't you see that if you don't tell me about yourself I'm always going to be an easy prey for people like her?' Dandy pleaded.

'All, right, I'll tell you,' he said with a sigh. 'I first met her soon after I graduated as an engineer. I was working for my Aunt Cécile's husband, Gervais Noyon. He owned a big construction company in France. I was young, impressionable. Nicole was beautiful, experienced, older than I and married to a man twenty years her senior who bored her to tears. She made love to me and I was flattered by her interest and for a while we used to meet regularly at an apartment she owned in Paris.' His twisted smile mocked himself. 'It was a purely sexual affair and for me, it was soon over. I stopped going to see her.'

'What did she do?' asked Dandy.

'I learned the hard way that one doesn't drop a woman like Nicole,' he replied wryly. 'She likes to call the tune in any extra-marital affair she has, that is why she prefers men younger than herself. But any man who gives her the brush-off, as I did, is made to pay.'

'How did she make you pay?'

'She made sure I was made the scapegoat in a scandal that involved her husband, herself and Gervais Noyon's Company. You see, the French Government granted the Noyon Company a big contract for the building of a dam in France. Noyon's competitors implied that pressure had been put on Jules Bujold, who worked for the department involved, to grant the contract to Noyon. They suggested that Nicole had been influenced by an employee of Noyon to pressure Jules. When Nicole was interviewed by the press she admitted that she had been asked by a Noyon employee to influence Jules and after a great show of reluctance agreed to name that employee.'

'You. She named you,' guessed Dandy.

'She named me,' said Yvan dryly. 'The news was headlined in the Paris newspapers and her revenge was complete when Gervais, who was really responsible for getting her to influence Jules, got out of the mess by giving me the sack.'

'Oh, how mean of both of them. How corrupt of them,' exclaimed Dandy.

'I agree with you, but it happens all the time in big business and political circles and it was a lesson I had to learn,' he said. 'But that was not all. My father was very angry when he read what had happened and said he would only forgive me for besmirching the name of Rambert if I would marry and settle down. He even went so far as to choose a bride for me. That did it. I told him I would get married only when I was ready. He told me to clear out and not return until I was married. I left France and came to Canada.'

'So Nicole wasn't lying when she told me why you and your father quarrelled,' Dandy said thoughtfully. 'She told me you had told her you were thinking of getting married the last time you saw her.'

'That is true, I did. To get rid of her. I told her I would be getting married but I didn't tell her about Anik.'

'She said it was because your father was putting pressure on you, that he'd threatened to cut you out of his will if you didn't marry soon, before he came to visit you,' said Dandy, watching him closely.

He stared at her frowningly for a few moments and then began to laugh.

'She did all she could, didn't she, to turn you against me, by telling you such lies?' he said scoffingly. 'My father has never threatened to disinherit me if I don't marry. Anyway what has he got to leave me in his will?'

'A considerable fortune and an estate in Normandy, Nicole said,' muttered Dandy, who was beginning to feel very foolish now for having listened to Nicole, and for believing what the woman had told her.

'But my father has no fortune. He has only his pension from the army. As for the estate in Normandy,' he began to laugh again, 'it is only an old farmhouse set in a few acres of apple orchards and he will probably leave it to my sister because her husband is a farmer.' He stepped towards her, put his hands on her shoulders and looked down into her eyes, his own softening and darkening. 'And now that I have told you everything about my regrettable association with Nicole and have explained about Niki, do you still feel you want to end our marriage? You know, what happened in my life before I met you is really none of your concern. It's all past, done with, and all that matters to me now is being with you.'

His hands slid caressingly down her back and he drew her against him. Bending his head he kissed her throat while pressing his fingers into her softly rounded buttocks and grinding her hips against his. When she felt the hard thrust of his maleness inviting her to even greater intimacy she caught her breath in a gasp of delight.

'I've missed you, Dandy, while I've been away, more than I would have imagined,' he whispered. 'And when I arrived back in Montreal and you weren't there and I found your note with your wedding ring I was angry and puzzled. I was trying to figure out what had happened when Douglas arrived and told me you were here. It seems your mother was worried about you and she asked him to contact me when he phoned her earlier this week to say he was coming here today. I was glad to see him and to come with him. And now I am here and I have been wanting you all afternoon. I must have you.' There was a thick urgency in his voice.

'No, wait. I have to know first if. . . .'

The words were cut off as his mouth covered hers. His kiss was like a flame touched to dry kindling. It ignited the time-bomb of her frustrated desire so that she responded eagerly, pressing against him greedily and opening her mouth to the invasion of his tongue.

'The bedroom,' he muttered thickly against her cheek, 'where we are going to sleep tonight. Where is it?'

'We must talk some more,' she replied pushing away from him. 'There's something I must know.'

'Then show me where we are going to sleep,' he replied.

'All right.'

Hand in hand they went up the stairs together and she led him along the landing past her bedroom to the one next to it, a guest room furnished with two single beds.

'Here, you are,' she said and slid past him back to the doorway. 'Goodnight, Yvan.'

Closing the door quickly she sped along the landing to her own room, grinning impishly. Into the room she ran and closed the door behind her, leaning on it with all her weight. But she couldn't stop him from pushing the door open, forcing it against her efforts to keep it closed. She sprang away from it and flattened herself against the wall, flicking off the switch on the wall so that the bedside lamp she had left on went out. The door swung inwards. He entered and kicked the door shut so that they were both trapped in a darkness that was only slightly relieved by starlight shining in through the window.

'I think I've caught you,' he whispered, laughing softly.

'Arrogant animal,' she hissed at him and began to slide along the wall away from him. 'You think you can come here, make a few explanations and then have your way with me. Well, you can't. Not until I'm ready and I'm not right now.'

'But you are, you are,' he said, coming after her. 'I've just kissed you and so I know you're longing for me to do this.' In the darkness his fingers found her breasts and their fingertips flicked lightly across them so that she gasped as sharp sensations zig-zagged through her. 'And this,' he added, stepping closer, his breath fanning her cheek.

Guessing that his arms were reaching for her she blocked them with a raised arm and whirled away from him. He followed her and she kicked out at him, then tripped over something and measured her length on the floor, all the breath knocked out of her. He was down beside her immediately, touching her shoulder gently.

'*Cherie*, are you all right? What happened? Why did you fall?' he demanded, his voice rough with concern. Taking hold of her he lifted her against him, cradling her in his arms. 'Ah, you know I would much rather kiss you than fight with you Dandy,' he whispered. 'And you know too that you would much rather be kissed.'

There was no longer any urge left in her to defy him, no defence against the tender touch of his hands. A long shaky sigh shuddered through her and she yielded to him, grasping handfuls of his hair and pulling his face down to hers.

'Oh, yes,' she moaned. 'I would much rather be kissed, but only by you, my dearest dear. Only by you. I've missed you terribly, too.'

She kissed him hard on the mouth to let him know that no matter what she had said to him he was really very welcome to take what he wanted, even though there was still something she wanted to know that he hadn't told her, because he was right, she was longing to receive him and to soar with him to the heights of passionate fulfilment.

It was a swift spontaneous mating, beautiful in its completeness, a satisfying by both of them of their own urgent needs, done in the dark on the soft bed and afterwards by the glow of the bedside lamps they worshipped each other's bodies until passion flared again, uniting them in a glorious burst of ecstasy, like a rocket exploding in a brilliant show of sparks. Then, all passion spent, they lay speechless, entwined together, sunk in rapturous languor, neither of them wanting to disturb the other until, at last, they both slept.

Dandy woke late. She was alone and bright yellow sunlight streamed into the room. The bedside lamps were off and there was nothing in the room to indicate that Yvan had slept with her, not even an article of his clothing.

A terrible sickening panic stabbed through her and she sat up quickly. The swiftness of her movement brought on another sickness, the now familiar morning sickness. Her hands pressed against her still flat stomach, she swallowed hard and lay back waiting for the feeling to subside.

Surely she hadn't imagined Yvan had been with her. But if he had been with her where was he now? Had he left her, taken what he had wanted and gone? Oh, no. *No.* Hastily she scrambled off the bed, grabbed her housecoat from the floor, slipped it on and fastened it. Still gagging a little on the nausea she hurried along the passage to the stairs, ran down them and went straight to the kitchen. The room was empty. Where was everyone?

She went to the fridge and took out fresh orange juice. She poured some into a glass and was drinking it when her grandfather came into the room, carrying an overnight bag.

'Ah, so you're up at last. How are you doing this morning?' he boomed heartily.

'Great. How are you?' she lied.

'Great, just great.' His dark eyes twinkled at her affectionately.

'I must have overslept,' muttered Dandy, pushing her hair behind her shoulders. 'Where is everyone?'

'Well, now, Morton's gone to the factory and Anne has gone shopping and it's Marcie's day off,' he replied seriously. She waited but he didn't mention Yvan. He just watched her gravely and she guessed, from past experience, that he was deliberately teasing.

'And Yvan?' she forced herself to say.

'Yvan?' He pretended to be surprised. 'Don't you know where he is? Didn't he tell you?'

'Oh, Gramps. Stop teasing. I'm not in the mood,' she sighed, slumping down in a chair at the table.

'Okay,' he replied. 'I'll tell you. He's gone jogging. I've said goodbye to him. I just have to say goodbye to you, young lazy-bones.' He put an arm about her shoulders and hugged her. 'I have to get on the road to New York. I've a dinner date with my publisher today.' He tousled her hair. 'I guess you'll be going back to Montreal and Yvan will go with you.'

'I guess so,' she murmured.

She went with Douglas to the front door and kissed him goodbye there, then went back to the kitchen. She supposed she should start making some breakfast. The trouble was the thought of bacon and eggs made her feel sick, but at least she could make some coffee.

She had just plugged in the coffee maker and was setting the table with table mats, cereal dishes and coffee mugs when Yvan came in through the back door. He was breathing hard and his shirt was damp with sweat.

'I'll take a shower and be with you in a few minutes,' he said striding straight through the kitchen and out into the hall, not stopping to kiss her as she was sure a loving husband would do.

The coffee had perked and she was trying to eat cereal when he came back, his hair wet and sleek, his skin glowing with health. In fact he looked so healthy and fit she felt jealous, and wished for a crazy moment that she wasn't pregnant and didn't feel sick.

'Would you like cooked breakfast?' she asked, feeling strangely nervous for some reason, hoping he would say no or would offer to cook it for himself, because she was sure she would be sick if she had to cook and she didn't want to betray to him the fact that she was pregnant.

'No, thanks. Cereal will be enough. And coffee.' He sat down at the table. 'What happened to you this morning? I felt sure you would want to go jogging, too, but when I tried to wake you up you refused to surface.'

'Oh, I don't know,' she muttered, pouring coffee for him, but none for herself.

'No coffee for you?' he asked.

'No. I . . . I don't want any.' She put the coffee pot down, avoiding his eyes. 'Gramps has gone,' she said, anything to distract him from pursuing the subject of her not drinking her favourite drink. 'Are . . . you . . . I mean . . . when do you have to go back to Montreal?'

He didn't say anything. There was only the sound of cereal being shaken into a dish and then the glug of milk being poured on it. Dandy looked across at him just as he looked at her. Across the space that separated them their eyes met warily.

'You haven't finished your cereal,' he commented, noting that she had pushed aside her half-full dish.

'No. I . . . I don't feel like eating any more. You haven't answered my question. When are you going back to Montreal?'

'And you haven't answered the question I asked you last night,' he retorted, ignoring his cereal and coffee, leaning his folded arms on the table and looked at her with narrowed eyes.

'What question?' she parried.

'Do you still want to end our marriage now that you know I have no lover except you?' he said, reaching out and covering one of her hands, which was resting on the table, with one of his own. The expression in his eyes changed from cool curiosity to warm blatant desire and she felt her pulses throb. Quickly she looked down at the lean hand covering hers. Gently his thumb began to caress her wrist.

'No,' she whispered. 'I don't want to end it, but . . . but what about you?' She looked at him challengingly. 'I only want to end our marriage if you do.'

'Would I have come with Douglas yesterday to see you if I wanted to end it?' he retorted softly. Rising to his feet he walked round the table to her and taking both her hands in his pulled her to her feet. 'I want you and only you,' he murmured, and began to draw her towards him. She braced herself against the pull of his hands, holding her ground and looking at him proudly.

'But you don't love me,' she said. 'You don't love me like ... like you loved Anik. Never once have you said to me, *Dandy, je t'aime*, not even in your dreams.'

He dropped her hands as if they burned him. Hostility glittered in his eyes. He turned away from her, picked up the coffee pot and poured more into his mug. He sat down at the table again. Slowly he looked at her. The glitter had gone from his eyes. He looked suddenly weary and bitter.

'If it is always going to be like this, if you are always going to fling my past in my face, it would be best if we did end our marriage,' he said flatly and coldly. 'You are right I do not love you like I loved Anik. I cannot love you like I loved Anik. . . .'

'Then go away. Go back to Montreal and ... and never come to me again,' Dandy flared angrily and began to rush blindly from the room, feeling the nausea curdling in her stomach. But she didn't get very far because Yvan sprang from his chair with such force he knocked it over and stepped in front of her. Taking hold of her shoulders he held them in a vice-like grip.

'Now wait and listen to me finish what I have to say,' he snarled at her.

'Oh, no ... I can't, I can't,' she cried wildly,

breaking free of his hold and running from the
room down the passage to the small washroom.

In the green-tiled, green-carpeted room she
leaned over the lavatory, retching painfully. The
spasm of sickness didn't last long, it never did, and
she was soon straightening up, pushing her hair
back and reaching for a cloth to wipe her face.

'Why are you sick?'

Yvan spoke just behind her and she turned. He
was leaning in the doorway, watching her from
under frowning brows.

'It ... it was the smell of the coffee,' she
muttered. 'I'm all right now. Excuse me, please I'd
like to go and get dressed.'

He stood aside and she walked past him, along
the hallway up the stairs to her bedroom. She was
quivering all over and wishing regretfully she
could unsay what she had said to him about Anik.

*You always hurt the one you love, the one you
shouldn't hurt at all.* The words of a popular ballad
she had heard as a child sang through her mind.
How true it was. She did nothing but hurt Yvan
by her outspokenness, and yet she loved him. It
was because she loved him so passionately and
possessively that she struck out at him all the time,
hoping to strike a spark of love in him for her,
perhaps?

She dressed in a summer skirt of printed cotton,
tiny flowers printed on a red background, which
had a flounce around the hem and was gathered
into a wide waistband. With it she wore a simple
white blouse. She strapped on sandals and then
brushed her hair. The gypsy-style clothes suited
her height and dark colouring and on sudden
impulse she took out the golden ear-rings, plain

circles of pure gold which her mother had given her once, but which she had rarely worn, and hung them from her ears.

When she went back to the kitchen Yvan wasn't there and she experienced again that sense of panic she always felt when he disappeared without telling her. Oh, God, she'd done it this time. He had left. She had told him never to come to her again so he had left and she would never see him again. Oh, what a fool she was. What a silly, rebellious fool. Hands to her face she sank down on a chair at the breakfast table, tears spilling from her eyes and down her cheeks, dripping over her fingers. So sunk was she in misery that she didn't hear footsteps behind her. Not until arms came around her and she was lifted from the chair did she know he was there and then her joy because he hadn't left after all broke through her pride and misery and she wound her arms around his neck and buried her tear-wet face against his neck.

'So what is this?' he asked, his voice deep and soft as he held her closely. 'Why are you crying?'

'I thought you'd gone,' she muttered, sniffling.

'You didn't hear the front doorbell ring?'

'No.' She pushed away from him. 'Who was it?'

'The mailman with a parcel for Anne.' He touched her face, wiping away teardrops with the tip of his finger. 'What is it, *chérie*? Why are you so sad?'

'I didn't mean what I said. I didn't mean it. I don't want you to go away, not without me. Oh, Yvan, I love you, I do really and truly but I can't bear to share you with another woman. I can't and I won't.'

'So will you listen to me while I finish what I was saying to you?' he asked, stroking her hair comfortingly. Her face against his neck again she nodded affirmatively and after a brief silence he said slowly, 'I cannot love you like I loved Anik, but that doesn't mean to say I don't love you at all.'

She lifted her head to look at him. Framing her face with his hands he kissed her gently and smiled at her.

'I do love you, Dandy. *Je t'aime*,' he murmured. 'I wouldn't have come to you and asked you to marry me if I hadn't discovered I had fallen in love with you while we were together in the cabin in Vermont.' He paused, frowning, then went on in a low voice. 'I was at a very low ebb emotionally speaking when I met you. Anik's death had hit me very hard and I was convinced I would never love a woman again. But your warmth and generosity that weekend woke me up from the numbed state into which I had fallen. I found comfort as well as pleasure in being with you, although I didn't realise it until I was back in Montreal. So when I could get away I came to find you again and to ask you to marry me.' He paused again then whispered, '*Dandy, je t'aime, je t'aime beaucoup* and I want to stay married to you. Please will you wear this ring again?'

She looked down. The platinum ring gleamed between his finger and thumb. She held out her left hand and he slid the ring on her third finger. Tears still glittered like stars in her dark eyes but she smiled through them, the warm melting smile which held so much charm.

'Thank you,' she said. 'Thank you for coming

here and telling me all that you have. I'll try to be good and not run away from you again.'

'And I'll try not to give you any reason to run away from me,' he promised, gathering her into his arms again.

They kissed for a long time, stopping only when they both needed to come up for air. Yvan said, with a wicked glint in his eyes,

'And now that I've told you all about myself and we are married again, isn't there something you have to tell me, something to do with sickness in the morning and a sudden dislike of coffee?'

'Oh,' she gasped, looking down her nose at him. 'You know far too much about women. Far too much.'

'Now, before you start accusing me of something I haven't done let me remind you I have a sister who has two children and also friends who have already become fathers and have told me all about their wives' strange behaviour during pregnancy,' he cautioned her. 'So, tell me. Is it true? Am I going to be a father too?'

'Yes, you are,' she admitted reluctantly. 'But I wish you hadn't guessed. I wasn't going to tell you.'

'Not tell me?' he demanded, his eyes narrowing dangerously.

'Not . . . not until I was sure you wanted to stay married to me because you want me and love me. I didn't want you to feel you had to stay married to me just because I'm going to have your child.' She became aware he was looking serious, almost worried. 'Oh, what's the matter? Aren't you pleased? Don't you want me to have your child?'

'It isn't a question of whether I want you to

have my child,' he replied. 'It's whether you want to have a baby.'

'But of course I do,' she insisted. 'And I'm going to eat all the right food and do all the exercises. I've been to the doctor and had all the tests and he says everything is perfect so far. He'll be a Christmas baby.'

'*He?*' He raised his eyebrows. 'Why not *she*? Would you like her to be born here?'

'I'd never thought *he* would be born anywhere else,' she confessed. 'You see I didn't believe you would come after me. I thought you ... you'd want to be with Nicole.' She saw his face darken angrily and rushed on. 'He can be born in Montreal.'

'But I might not be in Montreal next Christmas,' he said. 'The company have appointed me to that job in Colombia. We got the contract, you see, to build the dam.'

'Then the baby will be born in Colombia because I'll come with you and live with you there,' she asserted. 'When do we leave?'

'*I* leave in August, after my father has been to visit us.'

'*We* leave,' she argued.

'I think perhaps it would be best if you stay here in Renwick and had the baby here, where the hospital is good and you know the doctor,' he replied firmly.

'No,' she retorted rebelliously.

'Yes,' he insisted.

'Oh, you can't mean it. You can't expect me to stay here and let you loose among all those South America *señoritas*,' she said angrily. 'I won't do it. I won't. And if you love me as you say you

do you'll let me come with you. Oh, please Yvan.'
She flung herself against him, wrapping her arms
about him. 'You've got to let me come with you.
We'll never get to know each other any better, if
you don't.'

'It's because I love you and care for you that I
think it wiser for you not to come. I wouldn't like
you to lose the baby or be ill yourself because you
didn't have the proper care and attention. I could
not bear to lose you, Dandy. I couldn't bear it if
you died, too.'

'But it won't be like that,' she said softly,
touching his cheek with comforting fingers,
realising he was recalling the agony of spirit he
had suffered when Anik had been killed. 'I'm very
strong and having a baby should be the most
natural happening in the world for a woman. I'll
be all right.' He still looked unconvinced so she
pushed away from him and said with a sigh, 'Oh,
all right, I'll stay here if you prefer to go on your
own. I'm beginning to get the message. You don't
like having me around all the time.'

He didn't reply immediately and the minutes
slipped by in an agonising silence and she was just
beginning to think that she had hit on the truth
when he spoke quietly,

'Then you've been getting the wrong message. I
do like having you around all the time. I'm only
thinking of you. You might not like living in
Colombia for two years.'

'I'll like anywhere as long as I'm with you,' she
replied fiercely in frustration because once again
she had come up against that steel-like inflexibility
of his will. 'Oh, don't you understand? I want to
be with you always, go where you go, live where

you live. I want that more than anything else in the world, more than a career, more than a baby.'

She paused, watching him, hoping to see the steel door at the back of his eyes lift; hoping he would let her have a glimpse into the innermost depths of his heart, just for a brief moment, just so that she would know he felt as passionately about her as she did about him.

But his face didn't change and, feeling repulsed, she drew away from him and wandered disconsolately over to the kitchen window to stare out blindly, not seeing the greenness of trees, the blueness of the sky.

'All right,' she said again. 'I'll get by somehow, if you go away without me, but I'm warning you I'll only be half-alive. And . . . and when you come back . . . I might not be here.'

Her last words dropped like stones into a pool, each one conveying a subtle threat. He moved quickly, coming over to her and spinning her around to face him.

'And just what do you mean by that?' he demanded. Blue flames had begun to flicker in his eyes and she felt her pulses leap. Had she roused him at last?

'What I say,' she retorted. 'If you go away without me I can't promise to be here when you come back from Colombia. I love you and I want to see you every day or as often as possible for as long as we both live. I won't be left behind. I won't be left behind as my mother was left by my father.'

'Then assuredly you must come with me,' he replied, relenting suddenly. A faint mocking smile curved his lips, but not before she had seen something dark and tortured looking at her out of his eyes. 'For I would not like you to be going about half-alive. And if you weren't here when I came back. . . .' He broke off, pulling her against him, his arms going around her to hold her closely, effectively preventing her from seeing the expression on his face by burying it in the thickness of her hair. 'Don't let us talk any more about it, Dandy,' he said gruffly and then pushing her away a little he claimed her lips in a fiery kiss which, as always, melted all her opposition to him.

After a while he raised his head and looked at her without mockery, his manner very stern.

'But if you're going to come with me you must promise that you won't run away if problems come up—and they will. You must promise not to run away if sometimes we disagree or even quarrel, or if I do something you don't like. Love doesn't run away. It stays, keeps faith and faces up to problems, tries to solve them.'

'I think I've learned that now,' she whispered and then a mischievous grin curved her lips. 'And sometimes love asks damn fool questions, too,' she added teasingly.

'And sometimes it answers them, given time,' he retorted the wicked glint of humour back in his eyes as his lips hovered close to hers. '*Je t'aime, Dandy, je t'aime beaucoup*,' he said, passion deepening and roughening his voice. 'Always remember that and our marriage will last until the end of our days.'

'Until the end of our days,' she repeated and lifted her mouth willingly to his.

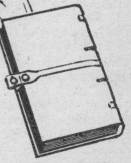

Take these
4 best-selling novels
FREE

Yes! Four sophisticated,
contemporary love stories
by four world-famous
authors of romance
FREE, as your
introduction to the Harlequin Presents
subscription plan. Thrill to **Anne Mather**'s
passionate story BORN OUT OF LOVE, set
in the Caribbean....Travel to darkest Africa
in **Violet Winspear**'s TIME OF THE TEMPTRESS....Let
Charlotte Lamb take you to the fascinating world of London's
Fleet Street in MAN'S WORLD....Discover beautiful Greece in
Sally Wentworth's moving romance SAY HELLO TO YESTERDAY.

*The very finest
in romance fiction*

Join the millions of avid Harlequin readers all over the
world who delight in the magic of a really exciting novel.
EIGHT great NEW titles published EACH MONTH!
Each month you will get to know exciting, interesting,
true-to-life people .... You'll be swept to distant lands you've
dreamed of visiting .... Intrigue, adventure, romance, and
the destiny of many lives will thrill you through each
Harlequin Presents novel.

Get all the latest books before they're sold out!
As a Harlequin subscriber you actually receive your
personal copies of the latest Presents novels immediately
after they come off the press, so you're sure of getting all
8 each month.

Cancel your subscription whenever you wish!
You don't have to buy any minimum number of books.
Whenever you decide to stop your subscription just let us
know and we'll cancel all further shipments.